W9-CIA-782

The Secret Lost at Sea

The sound of rapid footsteps on the wooden dock behind Nancy made her pause. She turned her head in the direction of the steps, but in the thick fog it was impossible to see.

Suddenly a bone-chilling scream rang out. The scream was followed by the splash of someone hitting the water, and a familiar voice cried, "Help!"

"George!" Nancy shouted as she raced down the dock. She spotted her friend swimming toward a ladder at the side of the dock.

"Are you all right?" Nancy asked as she gave George a hand up.

"Somebody pushed me from behind," George said as she climbed onto the dock. "I think he pushed me as a warning for us to back off the case. He said I'd better leave the seaport—and take my friend Nancy Drew with me!"

Nancy Drew
Mystery Stories

Available from MINSTREL Books

113

NANCY DREW®

THE SECRET LOST AT SEA

CAROLYN KEENE

EAU CLAIRE DISTRICT LIBRARY

86177

A MINSTREL® BOOK

PUBLISHED BY POCKET BOOKS

New York   London   Toronto   Sydney   Tokyo   Singapore

The sale of this book without its cover is unauthorized. If you purchased this book without a cover, you should be aware that it was reported to the publisher as "unsold and destroyed." Neither the author nor the publisher has received payment for the sale of this "stripped book."

This book is a work of fiction. Names, characters, places, and incidents are either products of the author's imagination or are used fictitiously. Any resemblance to actual events or locales or persons, living or dead, is entirely coincidental.

A MINSTREL PAPERBACK *ORIGINAL*

A Minstrel Book published by
POCKET BOOKS, a division of Simon & Schuster Inc.
1230 Avenue of the Americas, New York, NY 10020

Copyright © 1993 by Simon & Schuster Inc.
Produced by Mega-Books of New York Inc.

All rights reserved, including the right to reproduce this book or portions thereof in any form whatsoever. For information address Pocket Books, 1230 Avenue of the Americas, New York, NY 10020

ISBN: 0-671-79299-7

First Minstrel Books printing June 1993

10 9 8 7 6 5 4 3 2 1

NANCY DREW, NANCY DREW MYSTERY STORIES, A MINSTREL BOOK and colophon are registered trademarks of Simon & Schuster Inc.

Cover art by Aleta Jenks

Printed in the U.S.A.

Contents

1

Mystery at the Seaport

"Hey, Nancy, check out that huge sailing ship," George Fayne said to her friend Nancy Drew. "It's amazing!"

Nancy looked to her left and saw an old wooden ship that was at least a hundred feet long. Its three masts stood tall against the blue sky. A dozen old-fashioned square sails billowed in the warm summer breeze.

"We sure don't have anything like that back home in River Heights," Nancy said.

"I guess it helps to have an ocean around," George added with a laugh. "There aren't too many of those in the Midwest."

After flying to the East Coast that morning, the girls had just arrived at Bridgehaven Seaport, in Bridgehaven, Connecticut. All around them visitors were touring the charming buildings that re-created a typical seaport town. Other tourists were exploring the old sailboats moored along the Arcadia River and a lighthouse at the tip of a point of land.

Nancy looked down at the pamphlet she was holding. "According to this, the seaport has a lot more than just these exhibits from the old sailing days. There are also classes taught by experts in all seafaring fields and skills and a shipyard where they build and repair wooden sailing ships."

"Sounds great. I like this place already," George said with a grin.

Nancy wasn't surprised to hear that. With her tall, athletic build and short, curly, dark hair, George was crazy about everything having to do with sports and the outdoors.

"Too bad Bess couldn't come," Nancy said with a sigh. Bess Marvin, George's cousin, was on vacation with her parents in California.

"Yeah, but it's not as if this is a pleasure trip," George said. A grim look came into her brown eyes. "It's hard to believe that someone would want to wreck a place as nice as this."

Nancy nodded, brushing a lock of reddish-blond hair out of her face. "Mrs. Newcomb, the seaport's director, is really upset about the damage that was done to one of the exhibits," she said. "That's why she asked Dad if I could help find the person who's responsible."

Patricia Newcomb and Nancy's father, Carson Drew, had been friends since they were in college together. Over the years Mrs. Newcomb had heard of Nancy's reputation as a top-notch detective, and she'd asked for Nancy's help in finding the culprit.

"Oops," Nancy said, checking her watch. "We're supposed to meet Mrs. Newcomb at one o'clock, and that's three minutes from now."

"Let's go," George said.

The guard at the seaport entrance had given the girls directions to the building where Mrs. Newcomb's office was located. Picking up her red backpack and suitcase, Nancy followed a narrow path that led away from the river, past a row of old-fashioned buildings and what looked like a town square. Finally she and George reached a white clapboard building tucked away behind some trees. A sign by the door read Administration.

Inside, the girls found themselves in a house that had been converted into the seaport's offices. The foyer had nautical prints and paintings on the walls, and a reception desk was near the door.

"May I help you?" asked a dark-haired woman sitting behind the desk.

Nancy explained who they were, and the receptionist showed her and George to an office on the second floor. Inside, a woman with brown eyes and thick, shoulder-length chestnut hair was sitting behind a wooden desk. The woman was wearing a conservative linen suit, but her robust build and ruddy coloring gave Nancy the impression that she enjoyed the outdoors.

"Nancy Drew!" Patricia Newcomb exclaimed. She smiled warmly as she stood and shook Nancy's hand. "I'd know Carson's daughter anywhere—you have his blue eyes, I see."

"Guilty," Nancy said, grinning.

Mrs. Newcomb turned to George. "And you must be George Fayne. Thank you both so much for helping us out here at the seaport."

"We're happy to be able to come," George said sincerely.

Mrs. Newcomb sat down behind her desk, gesturing for Nancy and George to take the office's two other chairs. "I suppose your father told you that the seaport has recently been hit by a serious act of sabotage," she began.

Nancy nodded. "He didn't give me any of the details, though."

A frown darkened the seaport director's face. "A few nights ago someone damaged a display depicting life on board an old whaling ship. The display showed pictures of a whale chase and also re-created the crowded living quarters on board," she explained. "A valuable antique ship's clock was stolen from the display, but that's not the worst of it. Whoever took the clock also gouged the walls of the display with some words that were—well, let's just say I can't repeat them here."

4

"That's awful!" George exclaimed, shaking her head in disgust.

"Yes, it is," Mrs. Newcomb agreed. "Luckily the walls of the display don't have any historic value. But as you know, we have several irreplaceable historic sailing ships and a large collection of antique furniture, scrimshaw—designs carved into whale's teeth—and other crafts. Any damage to them could have a disastrous effect on the seaport."

"That's where we come in, right?" Nancy guessed.

Mrs. Newcomb nodded and gave Nancy and George an imploring look. "I hope you'll be able to catch the culprit before he does any more harm."

"Do you have any idea who's responsible?" George asked.

Mrs. Newcomb stared thoughtfully out the window for a moment before answering. "Every summer Bridgehaven Seaport offers a program for college students. It mixes courses in maritime fields with hands-on experience in activities such as sailing and boat building. The students live right here in Bridgehaven in houses owned by the seaport. They do all their own cooking and cleaning. It's a lot like staying in a dorm, except it's a more homelike atmosphere."

George's brown eyes lit up. "Sounds great." Then she frowned and added, "Oh—I get it. You think one of the students wrecked that display?"

"I'm afraid so," Mrs. Newcomb replied. "A few kids have been caught exploring the seaport after hours, which is strictly forbidden. They're allowed to use the seaport's library in the evenings, but that's it."

"Isn't there some kind of security system to make sure that students don't go where they shouldn't?" Nancy asked.

"We have guards, of course, but they can't be everywhere at once," Mrs. Newcomb replied. She went on to explain that students used a special gate to enter and leave the seaport after closing time. Each student had a key to the gate. "We lock up all the exhibits at night, but I'm afraid the locks are fairly simple."

She let out a sigh. "To be honest, we never had a problem before, so I never had any kind of alarm system installed."

Leaning forward, Nancy asked, "How can George and I help out?"

"I'd like you to pose as a student in the program, Nancy," Mrs. Newcomb said. "As it happens, we had a girl cancel out at the last minute, so no one will question your late arrival as her replacement."

She turned to George and added, "You'll sign on as an assistant in the shipyard—that's where new ships are built and old ones are restored. The tool used in the sabotage may have come from there. I've told the master shipbuilder that you're the daughter of a trustee who wants to learn the

6

craft of shipbuilding—that will explain why you don't have more experience. The students have workshops in the shipyard. I'd like you to keep an eye on them when they're there."

"Okay. I'll look for anything else suspicious, too," George promised.

"Good." Clapping her hands together, Mrs. Newcomb got to her feet. "I'll take you over to the shipyard now. Then Nancy and I can swing around to the Student Training Building—that's where the students in the maritime program go for their sailing lessons."

Mrs. Newcomb explained that she would arrange for the girls' bags to be brought to the houses where they would be staying. Nancy would be in one of the student houses. The director had arranged for George to stay in a private home where two girls who worked as guides at the seaport lived. Mrs. Newcomb indicated both houses on a map of Bridgehaven that was in Nancy's pamphlet. Then, after handing both girls their ID cards and keys to the student gate, she led them back out of the Administration Building.

As they made their way across the seaport, Mrs. Newcomb pointed out some of the sights. Narrow lanes wound around an old sailor's chapel, a schoolhouse, and a general store. A row of buildings running along the water re-created an old pharmacy, a workshop where wooden casks were made, and a store for nautical instruments.

After they passed a large village green, Mrs. Newcomb led the girls to a separate area dominated by an enormous wooden building with piles of wood stacked neatly outside. There were several wide doorways to the building, and Mrs. Newcomb stopped through the nearest one.

"Wow, this place is as big as an airplane hangar," George commented, looking around.

The inside of the building was one huge, open space. A long wooden ship's hull, propped up off the ground on supports, dominated much of the space. Several men and women were hard at work on it, scraping barnacles from the planking. At the far end of the building Nancy could see more carpenters constructing a small sailboat. Tools of all shapes and sizes were arranged on hooks against one wall.

Patricia Newcomb called out to one of the workers, a muscular man of medium height with dark hair and olive skin. A scowl came over the man's face when he saw her, and Nancy noticed that he took his time walking over to them. He didn't say anything, but simply crossed his arms over his chest and waited.

"Vincent, I'd like you to meet Nancy Drew and George Fayne," Mrs. Newcomb said, ignoring the man's sullen attitude. "Girls, this is Vincent Silvio, Bridgehaven Seaport's master shipbuilder." She went on to tell Vincent that George was a trustee's daughter who would be his new assistant.

8

Silvio gave George a dubious look. "So now I'm stuck with any old help you want to toss my way?" he asked Mrs. Newcomb bitterly.

George rolled her eyes at Nancy and bent close to whisper, "Nice guy."

Before Nancy could respond, Vincent Silvio took George's arm and led her toward the ship's hull, which was being scraped.

"Bye, George. I'll come by your house tonight after dinner," Nancy called after her friend.

Nancy wasn't sure what to make of Vincent Silvio. As Mrs. Newcomb led Nancy back outside, the seaport director said, "Vincent can be . . . difficult at times, but he's a top shipbuilder. Portuguese families like the Silvios have been sailing and fishing along this part of the Connecticut coast ever since the old whaling days in the early 1800s. Shipbuilding has been passed down from father to son in Vincent's family for generations."

"I never knew the Portuguese played such a big role in the old sailing days here," Nancy said as Mrs. Newcomb led her around the village green and out onto the point toward the lighthouse. To the right of the lighthouse was a low building alongside the water. Next to it a small dock jutted out over the river.

"This is the Student Training Building," Mrs. Newcomb told Nancy.

Half a dozen small sailboats were clustered in the water next to the dock, each manned by one or two students. Only one of the boats had its sails up, Nancy saw. A spindly, white-haired man was standing in the boat. He was wearing a work shirt with a pair of glasses sticking out of the pocket, and baggy blue pants that flapped around his legs. A blond boy in his late teens sat in the rear of the boat. He seemed to be helping the man demonstrate some sailing techniques.

"The older man is Cap Gregory, the sailing instructor," Mrs. Newcomb told Nancy in a low voice, pausing beneath the eave of the training building. "Let's wait here until he's done."

The warm summer breeze ruffled Nancy's hair. The seaport was just a few miles upriver from the coastline, where the Arcadia River spilled out into the Atlantic Ocean, and Nancy could smell a hint of salty air.

She listened while Cap Gregory explained to the students how to handle the sailboats during a race they were about to have. He pointed to two red buoys that were set up in the middle of the river, several hundred yards apart.

"You'll have to tack upwind, keeping your sails pulled close to the wind," he said. "Then, after circling around the far buoy, run with the wind to the near buoy. First boat to go back and forth five times wins the regatta."

Nancy had sailed enough to know that a regatta was a sailboat race. This one sounded like a lot of fun. She listened as Cap Gregory reviewed how to "come about," or turn the sailboat.

Cap was standing with his back to the blond boy who was in the sailboat with him. While the instructor spoke, the boy silently mimicked all of his gestures, causing some of the other kids to giggle. Cap was so caught up in his explanation that he didn't seem to notice, but Nancy caught the disapproving expression on Mrs. Newcomb's face.

"Okay, Deke," Cap said, turning to the blond boy. "Let's show them how it's done."

Deke made an exaggerated salute. "Yes, sir!" he replied in a voice that was anything but respectful. His eyes gleamed mischievously as he grabbed the lever that was used to steer the boat, pushing it hard to the right.

The little sailboat jerked around in a ninety-degree turn. The wind caught the side of the sail, sending it swinging around to Cap's side of the boat. Before Cap had time to duck out of the way, the sail smacked right into him, knocking him into the river!

2

Man Overboard

Nancy gasped and ran to the edge of the dock. For one awful moment she lost sight of Cap, who had disappeared into the Arcadia River. Then his head broke through the surface. He was sputtering, but he didn't look injured.

"That's the last straw, Mr. Ryan!" Cap declared angrily, treading water. "I want you out of my class—now!" Even in his sopping wet clothes, the white-haired man cut through the water with an easy grace as he swam back to the dock. The other students shifted nervously in their boats.

Nancy noticed that the defiant gleam remained in Deke Ryan's eyes as he maneuvered his sailboat the short distance to the dock and got out, securing the line to one of the moorings. He snickered at the sailing instructor, who now stood on the dock, water streaming down his face and clothes.

"I'd be nicer to me, if I were you," Deke sneered. "Unless you want to find all these boats at the bottom of the Arcadia River one day."

Mrs. Newcomb stepped forward. "That's enough, Deke. I want to talk to you, young man—in my office."

Despite the director's stern words, Nancy thought she seemed a little nervous. Deke was just a student—why would he make Mrs. Newcomb anxious?

The other students seemed surprised by the seaport director's sudden appearance. They looked on in silence while Mrs. Newcomb quickly introduced Nancy to Cap as a late arrival to the maritime studies program. Then the seaport director turned and left with Deke.

Cap didn't seem to mind at all that he was soaking wet. After calmly taking his glasses from his dripping shirt pocket, he put them on to look at Nancy. Then he welcomed her and found her a place in one of the sailboats.

As Nancy stepped into the boat, the petite girl sitting in it smiled at her. She was about Nancy's age and had penetrating blue eyes and curly black hair that was pulled back in a high ponytail.

"Hi," the girl greeted Nancy, smiling. "Mrs. Newcomb told me you'd be arriving today. I'm Claire Roebling, your roommate. And don't worry—despite what you just saw, most of us are pretty nice."

13

EAU CLAIRE DISTRICT LIBRARY

Nancy laughed. "Thanks for telling me. What's that guy's story, anyway?" she asked.

"Deke Ryan's a jerk. Don't pay any attention to him," Claire told her. "He's just mad because Cap got him and his roommate in trouble for climbing the rigging of the *Benjamin W. Hinton* at night, after the seaport was closed to visitors." She gestured toward the three-masted sailing ship Nancy and George had noticed earlier. "The old ships are strictly off-limits then."

Hmm, Nancy thought. If a troublemaking student was behind the sabotage at the seaport, Deke Ryan certainly would be a likely prospect.

"Anyone else would get kicked out of the program," Claire went on. "But Deke comes from an old New England sailing family. They've donated tons of stuff to Bridgehaven Seaport. Mrs. Newcomb wouldn't dare throw him out."

So *that* was why Mrs. Newcomb had seemed nervous about reprimanding Deke, Nancy realized. If the Ryans were big patrons of the seaport, they probably wouldn't be happy about their son getting in trouble.

"You can fasten that line at the bottom of the mast," Claire went on.

While the girls had been talking, Nancy had been raising the boat's triangular mainsail. Nancy fastened the rope where Claire indicated, then went to work raising the smaller sail at the front of the boat.

"What about you?" Nancy asked. "How did

14

you get interested in Bridgehaven's maritime program?"

Claire let out a short laugh. "Actually, I'm from Wyoming. I was never even on a sailboat until last fall, when I started college in Boston," she explained. "My roommate really loves sailing. The first time I went with her, I was hooked. I wanted to know everything about sailing and the old seafaring days, when sailing ships were a big deal in commerce and travel."

"Well, this is definitely the place to learn," Nancy said.

The other sailboats were lining up by the near buoy, Nancy saw. Claire took over steering the boat, while Nancy picked up the lines that controlled the two sails. A few minutes later Cap blew a whistle, and they were off!

Nancy had no difficulty following Claire's directions. Soon they were zigzagging upwind toward the far buoy. The wind whipped at Nancy's clothes and filled the sails as they skimmed across the blue-gray water. The feeling was so exhilarating that Nancy forgot all about the mystery that awaited her.

"Are you going down to the lighthouse to listen to the sea chanties?" Claire asked Nancy later that afternoon. The girls were just leaving the seaport's brick library, where the student program held its classes.

"You bet," Nancy replied, slipping her class

15

notes into her backpack. "Especially since that's what I'm doing my history project on."

After the regatta the students had gathered for the final class of the day, maritime history. Nancy learned that each student had to do a project for the class. Their teacher suggested that she do hers on old sea ballads, called sea chanties.

During the class, Nancy had discovered that Claire was a very serious student. Everyone else had spent time whispering about the regatta and kidding the winners—two boys named Greg and Julio. But Claire just took studious notes, glaring at anyone who interrupted the teacher. Nancy had to admire her dedication. It was obvious that Claire wanted to learn all she could in the program.

As the two girls made their way across the village green, Nancy could see that a group of tourists had already assembled next to the lighthouse. She recognized several other students from the program, including Deke Ryan. A handful of seaport employees stood in a semicircle, dressed in old-fashioned sailor's clothes. One of the employees held an accordion, and another had a harmonica.

Moments after Nancy and Claire joined the group, the accordion player gave a signal, and the singers launched into their first song: "Hoist every sail to the breeze, lads . . ."

Nancy couldn't help tapping her feet to the jaunty tune, which was all about catching a

16

whale. Some people in the crowd started clapping their hands to the beat. As the song went on to describe a chase with harpoons, Nancy could easily imagine the exciting scene.

Her attention was broken by a bitter voice to her left. "Those days are over for me," Cap Gregory muttered to no one in particular. "I'm through with the high seas—thanks to Patricia Newcomb."

Nancy studied Cap, who didn't realize she'd heard him. His sentimental expression hardened to a bitter glare. A few moments later he stormed off, disappearing around the other side of the lighthouse.

Nancy exchanged a look with Claire, who shrugged and whispered, "Cap says stuff like that all the time. He used to be the captain of a big sailing ship that the seaport sends around the world as a way of teaching people about sailing. I guess he wasn't too happy about retiring from the high seas," she added. "I think he had to because of his eyesight."

The girls returned their attention to the singers. The group had just started in on a new song, which seemed to be about a shipwreck:

"In eighteen hundred and forty-three,
My bonnie Mary was waiting for me.
When out of the North such a cold wind
    did blow,
My sweet Mary never again would I know. . . ."

17

A sudden movement high up in the lighthouse caught Nancy's gaze. She looked up in time to see a wide board balanced on the lighthouse railing, directly above where the singers were standing.

Nancy gasped as the board wobbled precariously, then slipped over the side. In a moment it would crash right down onto the singers' heads!

3

Trouble at the Lighthouse

"Look out!" Nancy cried, vaulting forward. Instinctively she grabbed her backpack by the straps and hurled it at the board with all her strength.

A moment later the backpack hit the board with a loud thud. The impact was just enough to deflect the board. It and the backpack clattered to the ground a few feet away from the singers.

Fearful cries rose up from the crowd, and people started to scatter. The singers stood in shocked silence.

"Wh-what happened?" asked one of them, a young man with sandy hair and a beard. "Where did that board come from?" He looked expectantly at Nancy.

Shading her eyes from the sun, Nancy stared grimly up at the lighthouse railing. "That's what I'd like to find out," she said.

19

Turning, she raced around to the lighthouse entrance. The cooler air inside the building made goosebumps stand out on her legs and arms. Nancy didn't see anyone in the small room at ground level, so she raced up the spiral stairwell that curved along the lighthouse's rounded walls.

She paused at the top of the steps, breathing hard. The stairwell opened into a round room surrounded by windows. It held a wooden table, some lanterns, and a small cot covered with a quilt. Several yellowed navigational charts were tacked to the wall. Bright light spilled into the room through the windows and an open doorway to Nancy's right. The sound of whistling came from the lighthouse balcony.

Moving stealthily, Nancy made her way to the doorway and peeked outside.

"Mr. Silvio!" she exclaimed, recognizing the master shipbuilder from earlier in the day. "What are you doing up here?"

The dark, muscular man was bent close to an area of the outside wall that had been stripped of its shingles. He was fitting a board over part of the space. At Nancy's question he put the board down and looked at her with curious dark eyes.

"The electricians were up here outfitting this old place with some new wiring," he said, nodding toward the fresh, plastic-coated strands threaded into the exposed space. "Someone's got to repair the damage they did to the outside wall.

Our regular carpenter's gone for the day, so it looks like I'm the man for the job."

He didn't seem to know anything about the fallen board. Or was that just an act? Nancy wondered. "One of your boards just fell over the railing," she explained. "It would have hit the singers if I hadn't managed to knock it away."

Vincent Silvio straightened up, his eyes flitting quickly to the lighthouse railing and then back to the piece of wood he'd just put down. "Wait a minute—I left that other board leaning up against the lighthouse wall, not against the railing," he muttered, half to himself. "How could it have fallen over?" His eyes narrowed as he looked back at Nancy.

"You're one of the students in the maritime program, right?" he asked. Before she could answer he continued angrily, "If you ask me, you're all a bunch of troublemakers. You probably threw that board over the railing yourself!"

Nancy bit back an angry retort. He had some nerve, accusing her like that. Or maybe Silvio was trying to deflect suspicion from himself. After seeing how angrily he had acted toward Patricia Newcomb earlier, Nancy thought it was possible that he was behind the sabotage to the seaport.

"You didn't see anyone else up here?" Nancy asked Silvio, without responding to his accusation.

The master shipbuilder glared at Nancy. "No

one—except you," he replied curtly. Then he returned to his work.

Nancy frowned at Vincent Silvio's back. She obviously wasn't going to get any more out of him. Going back inside the lighthouse, she took another look around.

"What's this?" she murmured, stepping over to a doorway she hadn't noticed when she'd first reached the windowed room. A small closet was set into the wall behind the stairs. Its door was slightly ajar. The closet held nothing more than a broom and some cleaning supplies, but it was big enough for someone to hide in.

Someone besides Silvio could have knocked the board over the railing while the shipbuilder was working, then hidden in the closet. The person could have sneaked out again while Nancy was talking to Silvio out on the balcony. Once outside, the person could probably slip into the crowd without attracting attention. Still, it couldn't hurt to ask around to see if anyone saw someone leave the lighthouse.

Nancy glanced back toward the balcony. She wasn't about to let Vincent Silvio off the hook yet. From now on she was definitely going to keep an eye on him.

"That's the best flounder I ever had," Nancy said after dinner that night.

"We get it fresh off the fishing boats when they

22

come into the commercial docks in downtown Bridgehaven," Claire explained.

Over dinner Nancy had gotten to know the four other girls besides Claire who shared the student house. Rochelle was a tall girl with dark hair and coffee-colored skin. Her roommate was a quiet, red-haired girl named Kristina. Nancy's other two housemates, Evelyn and Gayle, were both blond. They all seemed nice, but Nancy knew there was a chance that one of them was a saboteur.

The six girls had just finished doing the dishes and were relaxing in their living room. Brightly colored throw pillows offset the room's worn furniture, and the walls were decorated with cheerful posters.

Nancy reached for a handful of popcorn from a bowl on the coffee table. Trying to keep her tone casual, she said, "I heard someone wrecked one of the seaport displays here."

"Everyone thinks a student in our program did it, you know," Rochelle said, tossing a few kernels of popcorn into her mouth.

"You don't have any idea who it was, huh?" Nancy asked.

Gayle shrugged, resting her feet on the edge of the coffee table. "Not for sure. But after what happened when we were sailing today, I have a pretty good idea."

Gayle had to be referring to Deke Ryan, Nancy

thought. He had been near the lighthouse that afternoon, too. Unfortunately, none of the people gathered to hear the singing had seen anyone leave the lighthouse. Nancy was about to ask her housemates more about Deke when a voice called out from the front door.

"Yo, what's up?"

Nancy looked up to see a boy's muscular form silhouetted behind the screen door. The door opened, and Deke Ryan strode into the living room. He was followed by a thin boy with spiked black hair who wore a red T-shirt and baggy plaid shorts. Claire introduced him as Tom Chin. Nancy had found out during dinner that the boys were staying in another house owned by the seaport, just up the street.

As the girls called out greetings, Deke crossed the living room and perched on one arm of the couch. "Anyone up for some fun tonight?" he asked, reaching over to grab some popcorn.

"Just because you like to get into trouble doesn't mean you have to drag everyone else into it, too," Claire said, frowning at him.

"Oh, *excuse* me," he said sarcastically. "I forgot I was talking to Little Miss Bookworm."

Evelyn frowned, tugging on the end of her blond ponytail. "So maybe Claire *does* study a lot. It's not her fault that the rest of us are bigger goof-offs than she is."

Deke's blue eyes held a challenging gleam as he glanced around at the others. "Come on," he urged. "You can't get into trouble if you don't get caught."

Some of the girls giggled, but Claire let out a disgusted snort. "I've got studying to do," she told him. With that, she got up, grabbed her knapsack from the floor, and stormed from the house.

Tom shifted nervously from foot to foot. "Maybe we should stay low, Deke," he suggested. "Especially after what happened last time."

With a disappointed shake of his head, Deke said, "I guess I'm on my own." He got up and walked out the door with an arrogant swagger.

Nancy couldn't believe Deke was so proud of being a troublemaker. Maybe he was just putting on an act to get attention, but she didn't want to take any chances. If Deke was up to no good, Nancy was going to make sure she and George did all they could to stop him.

"I guess I'll head to the library, too," she fibbed, getting to her feet. She quickly said goodbye to her housemates and Tom Chin, then hurried out the door.

In the deepening shadows of dusk, Nancy headed down the narrow road that led to Arcadia Street, where the seaport was located. After consulting her map to see where George was staying, she made her way past the seaport entrance to a blue house a few streets down.

George was sitting on the front steps with two girls who wore shorts and blue Bridgehaven

Seaport staff shirts. Nancy guessed that they were George's housemates.

"Hi, Nancy!" George called out when she saw her. She turned and said something to the other two girls, then trotted over to Nancy. "Did you get any leads today?" she asked in a low voice.

"Two," Nancy replied, thinking of Vincent Silvio and Deke Ryan. "I want to stake out the seaport tonight to see if I can snare one of . . ."

Nancy's voice trailed off as she spotted a familiar figure across the street. The two-story building appeared to be a rooming house, with a porch running along the second floor and doorways dotting both levels. Cap Gregory had just emerged from one of the doors on the second floor.

Seeing him, Nancy suddenly recalled the way Cap had stormed off right before the board was shoved off the lighthouse. "Make that three suspects," she corrected. "Come on, I'll have plenty of time to tell you about them once we find a spot for our stakeout."

Ten minutes later Nancy and George were crouched next to a hedge near the docks. The seaport's main gate was locked now, but they had entered by way of the back gate Mrs. Newcomb had mentioned. In the darkness Nancy didn't think anyone would see them. The old-fashioned iron lamp posts didn't provide much light, but as Nancy's eyes adjusted to the darkness, she could make out several buildings and the docks where the antique ships were moored.

Keeping her voice at a whisper, Nancy told George about her suspicions of Deke Ryan, Vincent Silvio, and Cap Gregory. When Nancy told her friend what had happened at the lighthouse that afternoon, George's eyes filled with concern.

"Wow. So now it looks as if the saboteur is going after people, not just things," George said. "But I don't know if Vincent Silvio is the person we're looking for. He really seems to care about all the old ships here. Why would he wreck them?"

"I'm not sure," Nancy admitted. "But he doesn't seem to like Mrs. Newcomb. He sure gave her the cold shoulder at the shipyard this afternoon. Maybe he's—"

Nancy broke off as the sound of feet crunching on gravel came from somewhere nearby. She and George crouched lower behind the hedge.

When she saw the familiar spindly shape on the gravel walk, Nancy drew her breath in sharply. "Cap Gregory," she mouthed silently to George.

The captain walked past the girls' hiding place, then looked furtively around as he approached a wood-shingled building set back slightly from the water's edge. Cap put on his glasses and peered closely at the door. Then he pulled a pocketknife from his pocket, fiddled with the lock until it opened, and slipped inside.

"Nancy, what if he's going to damage something in there?" George whispered urgently. "We have to do something!"

Nancy's attention was suddenly diverted by a loud noise from the docks behind them. She whirled around, squinting toward the shadowy area surrounding the old ships moored there.

"Look, there's someone else," she hissed, pointing. George turned just as a dark figure bolted like a rocket from one of the ships.

Nancy didn't waste a second. "Stay here and keep an eye on Cap," she called to George.

Her feet pounded on the gravel as she tore after the figure. Nancy saw the person's head turn in her direction for just a second, but in the dim light she couldn't see who it was. Then the figure picked up speed, shooting in between two of the buildings across from the docks.

Breathing hard, Nancy skirted around a tree and shot into the small alleyway between the two buildings, where the figure had gone. She gasped as her toe caught on a root, sending her flying.

"Whoa!" she exclaimed, holding out her hands to break her fall. She hit the ground, then pushed herself quickly to a sitting position and tried to catch her breath.

The sound of the footsteps had faded. The person had gotten away!

Rising to her feet, Nancy brushed the dirt from her knees, then went back to find George.

"Whoever it was got away," she reported. "Is Cap still there?"

George shook her head. "He just left, but he wasn't carrying anything," she whispered. "I didn't want to look inside until you got back."

With a nod toward the docks Nancy said, "I want to check out that sailing ship first. The person who ran from it was definitely up to no good. It couldn't have been Cap, since he was in that building, but Cap could be working with someone else."

The two girls tried to make as little noise as possible as they walked back to the docks. Nancy was struck by the overwhelming feeling that someone was watching them, but she didn't see anyone. Shaking herself, she turned her attention back to the boat.

The sailing ship had two masts, Nancy saw. A sign on the dock said that it was the *Westwinds,* a fishing schooner from the late 1800s. The wooden planks of the ramp squeaked under the girls' feet as they walked up to the deck. Once there, Nancy paused to let her eyes adjust to the dimness of the space. Then she and George began searching for anything that looked unusual.

"No damage up here," George announced a few minutes later. She pointed to a raised cabin near the rear of the ship. "The stairs over there lead below."

The girls descended a set of narrow, steep

29

stairs. A shaft of moonlight filtered through the doorway, throwing a faint yellow glow over the area near the stairs.

Nancy paused at the foot of the stairs as her gaze fell on a wooden box that lay upside down on the floor. It was very ornate and decorated with gold wire in an intricate design. Bending down, Nancy turned the box right side up and opened the lid.

"Oh, no!" George exclaimed.

The box looked like a portable writing desk with several compartments built into it. The lid was lined with a rich, shimmering, reddish-orange fabric, but the fabric had been savagely shredded!

"We'd better tell Mrs. Newcomb about this right away," Nancy said grimly.

Suddenly George grabbed Nancy's arm. "Nancy, do you hear that?" she whispered.

Nancy froze. Someone was on the deck of the *Westwinds!* Before she could even think about looking for a hiding place, loud footsteps pounded down the stairway and a blinding light shone in her eyes.

"Hold it right there!" a deep voice growled.

4

Caught!

Nancy felt a sinking sensation in the pit of her stomach. Blinking into the bright light, she saw a beefy man in a guard's uniform. As he shone his flashlight on the damaged writing desk, she got a better look at his round, fleshy face and thinning brown hair.

"Caught you red-handed this time," he told Nancy and George, looking at them with steely gray eyes. "Mrs. Newcomb will have your heads when she sees what you've done to the captain's writing desk."

"Hey, we didn't do that," George said defensively, nodding toward the ripped lining. "We were trying to catch the person who did."

"Yeah, right. Tell me about it," the guard scoffed. He wore a dubious expression as Nancy and George explained what had happened.

"Patricia Newcomb asked us to come here to

find out who's been sabotaging the museum," Nancy finished. "Call her if you don't believe us."

The guard crossed his arms over his chest, looking from Nancy to George and back to Nancy. Finally, he pulled a police-type radio from his belt and spoke into it.

Nancy exchanged a frustrated glance with George. She was beginning to think that solving this case was going to be anything but easy.

"Boy, am I glad Mrs. Newcomb was able to straighten everything out," George said a few hours later. She and Nancy lingered outside the seaport's back gate, talking over the evening before heading to their different houses.

"Me, too," Nancy agreed. "For a while, I was afraid the guard was going to call the police."

The seaport director had come to the *Westwinds* as soon as the guard called her. After she had examined the writing desk, they had all gone back to the security office to fill out a report. The guard hadn't been pleased to learn that Nancy and George really weren't the saboteurs. He had agreed to give the two girls the full support of the seaport security force, but only because Mrs. Newcomb insisted.

"Mrs. Newcomb didn't seem very happy to learn that Cap Gregory was sneaking around in that building," George went on.

32

"I'm just glad that he didn't wreck anything," Nancy said.

After leaving the security office, the two girls and Mrs. Newcomb had returned to the building where Nancy and George had seen Cap. The display inside featured the belowdecks that had been salvaged from a commercial ship called the *Arcadia Queen.* The intricate, carved-wood paneling in the display hadn't been damaged, but Nancy was still in the dark as to what Cap Gregory had been doing there.

"Mrs. Newcomb did confirm what Claire told me, that Cap was forced to retire from sailing the high seas because his eyesight didn't meet the seaport's standards for captaining a ship," Nancy told George.

"And from what you and Claire heard at the lighthouse this afternoon, he's definitely bitter about it," George put in. "Mrs. Newcomb said she was going to talk to Cap about his attitude. Maybe she'll find out that he's responsible for the damage, and the case will be solved."

"I hope so." Nancy stifled a yawn, then glanced at her watch. "It's after ten-thirty. I think we'd better call it a night."

After saying goodbye, George continued down Arcadia Street toward the house where she was staying. Nancy turned up the side street that led to her student house.

The living room was filled with kids when she

33

arrived. All her housemates were there, as well as Deke, Tom Chin, and two other boys. As soon as they saw her, everyone fell silent. Nancy had the uneasy feeling that they'd been talking about her.

"Um, hi, everyone," she said.

No one answered. After a moment Deke Ryan held up a glass of lemonade he was drinking. "Here's a toast to Bridgehaven Seaport's newest criminal—Nancy Drew!"

Nancy stared at him, dumbfounded. She wasn't sure what was going on, but she didn't like it. "What are you talking about?" she asked when she finally found her voice.

It was Claire who answered. "Come off it, Nancy. Deke told us all about how the guard caught you after you wrecked that captain's writing desk. I can't believe I thought you were nice." Claire's voice was angry, and her blue eyes held an icy glare. The other kids were also looking at her as if they didn't trust her.

"I didn't do that," Nancy protested. She instinctively opened her mouth to defend herself— then clamped it shut again. Whatever happened, she couldn't blow her cover.

"Look, I admit I got caught on the *Westwinds.* It's such a great boat, I couldn't resist exploring a little," she fibbed. "But the desk was already ruined when I got there. Besides, I didn't even get to Bridgehaven until today—*after* the ship's

34

clock was taken and the whaling display was damaged."

She looked around the room, trying to gauge the expression on the other students' faces. It was obvious that none of them believed her.

Nancy's eyes narrowed as they landed on Deke. He returned her gaze without flinching. She couldn't help wondering how he knew she had gotten in trouble in the first place— unless he had been somewhere nearby himself. Deke Ryan was looking more and more like her top suspect.

The following morning before her first class, Nancy went to the Bridgehaven Seaport Bookstore to get the textbooks she would need for the maritime program. The bookstore was located among a cluster of buildings just outside the booth where visitors paid to enter the seaport. Nancy passed a gift shop and an art gallery and then went into the bookstore.

She paused inside the entrance and looked around. Display tables were set up in the open area near the entrance, featuring big books with glossy pictures of sailboats and seascapes. Around the sides of the room, wooden shelves had been arranged to create small nooks, each holding books for a different subject. A circular stairway to the left curved up to a balcony that was also filled with bookshelves.

A woman with brown hair and bangs stood behind the cash register next to the door. When Nancy asked where she could find the textbooks for her program, the woman directed Nancy to an area of the balcony that was opposite the staircase.

Nancy thanked the woman and went up to the area the woman had indicated. Sure enough, the textbooks were stacked in piles on a table there. She began working her way around the table, taking one of each.

"If I were you, I'd go for a cedar lapstrake construction," came a voice from somewhere nearby. "That'll give you a strong, light boat."

Nancy's head jerked up as she recognized Vincent Silvio's voice. Apparently he was in the next nook, the area on sailboat design. He seemed to be talking to someone else about building a boat.

"I was thinking the same thing myself," said a second, deeper voice. "What design do you recommend?"

"My own twenty-foot racer is as sleek a boat as you'll ever hope to find," Silvio said confidently.

There was a pause before the other person spoke again. "What about Pat Newcomb's new design—the Windseeker? I've heard those are doing quite well."

Suddenly the air crackled with intensity. "Patricia Newcomb never designed a boat that could

36

even float well, much less win a race," Vincent Silvio boomed in an outraged voice. Nancy was startled at how bitter he sounded.

"The only reason the Windseeker is selling is that *I* created it," Silvio went on angrily. "That dirty thief Newcomb stole my design!"

5

An Angry Shipbuilder

Nancy listened in shocked silence to Vincent Silvio's outburst. A moment later she saw him stalk around the balcony to the circular stairs. His fists were jammed into his pants pockets, and a scowl darkened his face. He drummed angrily down the steps. Then the door to the bookstore opened and slammed shut, and he was gone.

What a temper, Nancy thought. She peeked around the bookshelves in time to see a blond man walking after Silvio. Nancy heard him mutter, "Some people!" before he took a thin book down to the woman at the cash register.

Now at least she knew why Vincent Silvio hated Patricia Newcomb so much. Nancy hadn't realized before that they both designed sailboats. Silvio obviously thought that Mrs. Newcomb had stolen one of his designs.

This put a whole new angle on the case, Nancy

38

thought as she finished collecting the books for her courses. She would definitely have to talk to Mrs. Newcomb and find out more about the rivalry between her and Vincent Silvio. She supposed it was possible that the seaport director *had* stolen his designs. Still, that didn't justify wrecking the seaport's valuable displays.

Nancy did a double-take as she glanced at her watch. Maritime literature class started in just five minutes! Her questions would have to wait.

By the end of the morning Nancy's head was swimming. The maritime literature class had studied *Moby Dick*. Then, in marine science class, the instructor reviewed the scientific research techniques the class would be using the next day. The group was going to spend the day on the *Seafarer*, a one-hundred-foot research sailing ship.

The classes had taken place in a conference room in the library, with Nancy and the other students sitting around a large round table. As everyone gathered up their books, Nancy turned to Rochelle, who was sitting next to her.

"I can't wait for tomorrow's trip," she said. "I've never been on a sailboat that big before."

"Mmm," Rochelle said, barely looking at Nancy. She turned to say something to one of the boys in the class, ignoring Nancy completely.

With a sigh Nancy got up and left the library. The other kids in the maritime program seemed to be convinced that she was bad news. She hated feeling like an outcast, but at least the other students wouldn't question her when she spent time away from them on the case. Nancy decided to find George to talk about Vincent Silvio's outburst.

When she got to the shipyard, Nancy saw that George was feeding a board lengthwise into a big table saw. A young man wearing jeans, a staff T-shirt, and a leather work belt was supervising her.

Nancy waited until the board had been cleanly cut before she went over to her friend.

"Hi, Nancy. What's up?" George greeted her, taking off her safety goggles and brushing sawdust from her T-shirt and cutoff jeans.

"Not much," Nancy said. She didn't want to bring up the case in front of George's coworker. "Can you take lunch now?" she asked.

George looked expectantly at the young man, who glanced at his watch. "No problem," he said. "I'll let Silvio know. Oh—and if you're looking for the greatest hero sandwiches in the Northeast, try Augie's. It's right on Main Street."

The young man gave her directions. Then, taking the board she had cut, he headed for the other side of the shipyard building.

George got her shoulder bag from a row of lockers near the door, and she and Nancy left the seaport. After walking the few blocks to the main street of Bridgehaven, they turned onto it and

40

crossed over a drawbridge that spanned the Arcadia River. Looking upriver, Nancy could see the masts of the *Benjamin W. Hinton* back at the seaport. Downriver were commercial docks, where shrimpers and other fishing boats were moored. Straight ahead, stores and restaurants stretched along both sides of the main road.

Augie's was an informal sandwich shop about halfway down the block. The two girls ordered heroes and some sodas at the deli-style counter, then sat at one of the small tables.

Once they were seated, George studied Nancy and raised an eyebrow. "I can tell by that look in your eye that something else has happened, Nancy," she said. "Are you going to tell me what it is?"

Nancy laughed. "You know me too well," she said. Then, becoming more serious, she told George what she had overheard at the bookstore.

"Wow," George said when Nancy was done. "Silvio was fuming about something when he got to the shipyard this morning."

George took a bite of her hero, her brow furrowed in concentration. "He complained to one of the guys that Mrs. Newcomb stole some design of his that's turned out to be a hit with small boat builders. Apparently they both sell the designs in a store here in town."

"I'm not sure if he's just being paranoid, or if she really did steal his designs," Nancy said. "I guess I'll have to ask Mrs. Newcomb about it, but

41

I'm not looking forward to bringing up such a touchy subject. Did Silvio say anything about wanting to get back at Mrs. Newcomb?"

George shook her head. "Not that I heard."

"It could be an important lead," Nancy said, taking a sip of her soda. "We're already here in town. What do you say we try to find that store?"

"I'm game," George agreed.

The two girls quickly finished their sandwiches, then hurried back out to the street. They continued down the stretch of gift stores, clothing boutiques, and small restaurants.

"Over there," George announced, pointing across the street.

"Bridgehaven Wooden Boats," Nancy said, reading the sign above the storefront George had indicated. The window featured an elegant small-scale wooden sailboat, rigged with two sails.

She and George quickly crossed the street. Pushing through the door, they found themselves in a bright, airy store filled with woodworking tools, rudders, and other boat parts. Displays along two walls were filled with designs for sailboats. A middle-aged man with a short-sleeved shirt stretched taut over his potbelly stood behind a counter against the right wall.

"Excuse me," Nancy said, going over to him. "I'm looking for a design by Patricia Newcomb. I think it's called the Windseeker."

42

"Hey, didn't Vincent Silvio design that boat?" George said, giving Nancy a secret wink.

Good going, George, Nancy thought. If there was anything to Silvio's claim, perhaps the store owner knew about it.

The man behind the counter let out a chuckle. "Vincent Silvio would love to claim all of Pat Newcomb's designs as his own, but there's no truth to it," he said. "There tends to be a lot of jealousy among boat designers."

Moving from behind the counter, he crossed over to the display of designs and plucked out a plastic package. "Here you go. The Windseeker, by Pat Newcomb," he said, handing it to Nancy.

"Not that Vincent doesn't make a fine boat himself from time to time," the man went on. His finger slid over the display until he found a second design package, which he passed to the girls. "This twenty-foot racer is one of the nicest, fastest little boats I've ever been on."

Nancy was only half listening. Her attention was focused on the picture of a sleek, small sailboat on the front of the second package. Flipping it over, she saw that there was a chart that gave the dimensions of the boat and some other statistics. A boxed-in notice at the bottom of the package read, "For other designs by Vincent Silvio, write to . . ." It gave an address at 48 Elmwood Street in Bridgehaven.

Nancy elbowed George in the side, pointing to

43

the address. Maybe it was time to visit Vincent Silvio's house and see if they could find evidence of the seaport sabotage there!

A moment later, the girls were on their way. Following the directions the store owner had given them, they soon found themselves on a residential street a few blocks from Main Street. Number 48 was a narrow, two-story red house with a steeply sloped roof. Nancy was relieved to see that there was no car in the driveway.

She and George crept around to the back of the house. Nancy pressed her face to the window of the back door and stared into an empty kitchen. "The coast is clear," she told George. "At least so far."

The door was locked. Nancy pulled her wallet from her jeans pocket, took out a credit card, and went to work on the door. A few moments later she heard a click and pushed the door open. She and George slipped inside.

For a moment they stood listening. When Nancy didn't hear anything, she started toward the front of the house, gesturing for George to follow her.

"If you were Silvio, where would you hide a ship's clock?" Nancy whispered as they walked quietly down a short hallway toward what was obviously the living room. A flowered couch was set up against one wall, facing a TV set. The wall was lined with framed blueprints of sailboat designs. Nancy guessed that they were boats

Vincent Silvio had designed himself. An arched doorway on the other side of the room led to the front hallway.

George shrugged. "I don't know. Maybe—"

She broke off as the front doorknob rattled.

"Nancy!" George hissed, a look of panic in her eyes. "It must be Silvio!"

Nancy gulped as she heard the sound of a key scraping in the lock. She and George were going to be caught red-handed!

"We'll have to tell Mrs. Newcomb about it," Nancy said, nodding. She glanced at her watch. "That'll have to wait until later, though. Right now I've got to head to the *Benjamin W. Hinton* for a sail handling demonstration. It starts in about ten minutes."

As they crossed back over the drawbridge, Nancy glanced upriver at the seaport buildings. A reddish-brown corner of the shipyard building was just visible behind a stand of trees.

As Nancy gazed at the building, a thought occurred to her. "Do you know which locker at the shipyard is Vincent Silvio's?" she asked George.

George nodded. "Sure. It's got his name on it." Then a glimmer of understanding lit up her eyes. "You're not thinking of checking it out, are you?" she asked anxiously. "I mean, what if he comes back and surprises us *again*?"

"We'll just have to hope that he doesn't," Nancy said firmly.

The walk back to the seaport took only a few minutes. When the two girls entered the shipyard building, Nancy was relieved to see that only two carpenters were there. They were working on the boat shell she had seen earlier, on the opposite side of the building from the lockers.

Stepping over to the lockers, Nancy saw that several of them were labeled with name stickers. "Silvio" was printed on the top left locker in faded, scratched paint. There was no lock on the

48

and Claire. "Were you just sightseeing?" he asked mockingly. "Or planning your next attack?"

Nancy shot him an indignant glance. "Look, I wasn't even here when that ship's clock was taken, and I don't appreciate—"

"Ahem!"

Nancy turned to see Cap Gregory standing right behind her, his hands on his hips and a disapproving look in his eyes. "All right, crew, settle down," he said. "We're here to learn about sail handling, not to bicker. Mr. Ryan, with your family's distinguished sailing background, I would think you'd know that."

Deke just shrugged, but Nancy could feel the heat rise to her cheeks. She and the other students listened while Cap gave them a tour of the old whaling ship.

First he showed them four small whaling boats that hung from curved rails arching over the ship's railing. They could be lowered into the water at a moment's notice if a whale was spotted, Cap explained. Nancy cringed when she saw the *Hinton*'s huge blubber hook and the iron vat that was used to boil down the blubber into whale oil right on deck. After the blubber and tusks were taken, the whale's carcass was left at sea.

"I had no idea whaling was so gruesome," Kristina commented, crinkling up her face in distaste. From the looks on the other kids' faces, Nancy guessed that they shared her feeling.

"Whalers were no place for the squeamish," Cap said. "The men who handled this ship were hardened sailors. They wouldn't think twice about climbing the masts with gale winds pitching the ship in all directions." He eyed the group disdainfully. "But I guess even you landlubbers ought to be able to handle a trip up to the sails on a calm day like today."

It was obvious that Cap thought they were anything *but* the kind of seasoned sailors he had just mentioned. Nancy was determined to show him that she had what it took to do the job. She listened carefully while Cap explained that the students would be separated into two groups. Each group would climb up and unfurl one of the square sails, and then refurl it.

Cap pointed up the forward mast. Nancy noticed four wooden crosspieces to which the sails were attached. Cap called them "yardarms." The sails weren't hanging free but were fastened to the yardarms with canvas ties. The two lowest crosspieces had been set about five feet apart, some twenty feet above the deck.

Netted rigging angled up to the mast from either side of the deck in two strips that looked a little like rope ladders. Cap explained that the students would climb the rigging to the lowest yardarm, then reach up to the higher crosspiece and unfurl its sail.

Claire, Tom Chin, Evelyn, Rochelle, and a boy named Greg were in the first group, with Deke as their leader. Cap called instructions as the students clambered up the web of rigging and spread themselves out along the lower crosspiece.

Deke was standing at one end of the yardarm. When Cap gave the signal, the students untied the stops that bound the sail. Nancy saw that it was a far reach—most of the students grabbed on to the yard and nearby rigging for support. Finally the square sail dropped, filling with wind.

It took Deke's group several minutes to refurl the sail. After they had climbed back down to the deck, Cap went up to check their work. He tightened a few of the ties, then climbed down and sent Nancy's group up.

Nancy felt an exhilarating rush as she clambered up the webbed rigging to the lower yardarm. Even though the ship was anchored, it moved slightly, making her feel a little giddy. Just thinking about what it must be like for sailors to climb up in a storm made her stomach flip-flop.

When she reached the lowest crosspiece, she carefully made her way to the edge. The other five students spread out evenly next to her.

"Okay, let's untie the canvas stops now," she told the others when Cap gave the okay.

Nancy had to stretch to reach the tie closest to her. In order to give herself a little more leverage, she grabbed on to the netted rigging with one hand, reaching up with the other.

Suddenly there was a ripping sound, and Nancy felt the rigging give way. She gasped as she felt her hand flail wildly in the air, throwing her off balance. Her foot slipped, and she pitched downward toward the deck!

In one dizzying glance she saw a swirl of faces on the deck below—and the sharp point of the huge blubber hook directly below her!

7

Danger on the Whaling Ship

Nancy's heart leapt into her throat as she plummeted downward. She closed her eyes tightly but couldn't block out the image of the deadly hook below. Desperately she threw her arm out, trying to grasp something, anything. To her amazement, her hand caught on some more rigging, and she clenched her fist tightly around it. Her slender body jerked to a halt, then swung gently in the air.

When she dared to open her eyes again, Nancy saw that she was just a few feet above the ominous, iron blubber hook. Below her, her classmates all had looks of horror frozen on their faces.

Nancy tried to control the nervous tremor in her voice as she assured everyone she was okay. Taking a deep breath, she swung her feet around until they caught on the web of rigging. Then she climbed down to the deck, trying not to look at the iron hook a few feet to her left.

When Nancy reached the deck, the entire ship exploded in a chorus of anxious voices: "Are you okay?" "That was a close one!" "What happened?"

At least the other kids don't seem mad at me anymore, Nancy thought. They all looked worried. Even Deke had lost his smug expression.

"Nice save, Nancy," Cap said, appearing at Nancy's elbow. "What happened up there?"

Good question, Nancy thought. "I grabbed on to some rigging," she began, thinking out loud. "I think it ripped from my weight."

Cap craned his head to look up at Gayle, Kristina, and the three guys who were still twenty feet above them. "As you can see, it's only too easy to slip," he called. "If Miss Drew had been out on the water, there's a good chance she would have pitched over the side and been lost at sea."

Nancy gave Cap a sharp look. There seemed to be a glint of satisfaction in his deep blue eyes, though she wasn't sure why. Were his words meant to be a threat? Now that she thought about it, the way the rigging had suddenly given way didn't seem right to her. A boat's rigging wasn't meant to just snap like that, unless it had rotted or . . .

Nancy didn't like the thought that had just occurred to her. With a determined glance up at the others in her group, she said, "I'd like to give it another shot." Before Cap could stop her, she started climbing back up the rigging.

Her real purpose wasn't to show Cap that she wasn't afraid. Nancy wanted to get another look at the rigging that had given way.

The other students in her group, who were still on the rigging, made encouraging comments as she worked her way around them. Within moments she was back in the same spot where she had been standing before her fall. She took a close look at the rigging—then drew her breath in sharply.

The rope ends weren't rotted. They weren't frayed, either, the way they would have been if they had snapped from the stress of her weight. They had been cleanly sliced through. Someone had purposely cut the rigging!

"Nancy, are you all right?"

Nancy looked over to see Gayle staring at her expectantly. She and the others were obviously waiting for her to resume unfurling the sail.

"Uh, yeah, sure." Taking a deep breath, Nancy started talking the others through the procedure, but her mind wasn't on her work. Questions kept running through her head. Who could have sabotaged the rope? Cap had inspected the work just before her group had gone up. Had he cut the rigging to warn her off the case? How could he know her real purpose at the seaport?

Then again, Deke had been the previous

group's leader, and he had stood in the same spot. Nancy still didn't know if he was up to no good at the seaport, or if his cocky, mischievous attitude was all an act. But if Deke *was* the saboteur, it was possible that the reason he kept taunting her was to deflect everyone else's suspicions away from him.

Nancy shuddered as she glanced down at the blubber hook again. Whoever had cut the rigging wasn't just sending her a warning. It looked as though the person wanted her out of the way for good. From now on she was going to watch her back.

"Nancy, you could have been seriously injured in that fall," Patricia Newcomb said worriedly. As soon as the sail furling demonstration ended, Nancy had gone to the director's office to fill her in on what had happened. "I never would have asked your father for your help if I had known—"

"I'm all right. And luckily, no one else was hurt, either," Nancy assured her quickly. "I just keep thinking that if someone went to the trouble of trying to hurt me, I must be getting closer to figuring out who's sabotaging the seaport."

Mrs. Newcomb didn't look convinced. Before she could object further, Nancy said, "I'm beginning to wonder if Cap Gregory and Vincent Silvio might be working together. We already know that Cap is upset about having to retire from captaining sailboats on the high seas. And Vincent Silvio's motive might have something to do with" —Nancy took a deep breath before continuing—"a competition between you and him over sailboat designs."

The seaport director's eyes narrowed as Nancy related the story of Silvio's outburst about the design he thought Mrs. Newcomb had stolen.

"Not *that* old story again," the seaport director said with a sigh. "Vincent and I have been designing small sailboats for as long as I can remember. Once, about six years ago, we both happened to design small racers that were strikingly similar. For some reason, Vincent claimed that I stole that design from him."

Mrs. Newcomb shook her head ruefully. "Now every time I design a new sailboat, he makes the same accusation—that the design was his and I stole it. Nancy, I give you my word that all of my designs are Patricia Newcomb originals. If Vincent says otherwise, it's just because he's too jealous to admit that I'm the better designer."

That backed up what the owner of the wooden boat shop had told Nancy and George. From the slightly smug look on Mrs. Newcomb's face, Nancy could tell that she enjoyed being the winner in the competition with Vincent Silvio. "Maybe he resents your success enough to do damage to the seaport," Nancy suggested.

The seaport director shook her head. "Vincent may get hot under the collar when my designs do well, but I'm sure he doesn't really mean me any harm," she said firmly.

"I'm not so sure of that," Nancy said. She told Mrs. Newcomb about finding the scrap of fabric from the captain's writing desk behind Silvio's locker, and about seeing him with the ship's model.

"A ship's model?" Mrs. Newcomb repeated, raising an eyebrow. "As our master shipbuilder, Vincent is allowed to borrow from the collection of models. Sometimes he uses the models as reference for restoring old ships. If he followed official policy, I'll be able to track it down."

Nancy waited while the seaport director turned to the computer terminal on her desk and typed a series of commands.

"Vincent followed procedure, all right," Mrs. Newcomb announced a few moments later. "The ship's model he borrowed is from the *Arcadia Queen.*"

Nancy frowned. "The display Cap snuck into last night was from the *Arcadia Queen,* too, right?" she asked.

Mrs. Newcomb nodded grimly. "Maybe you're right about the two of them working together. But what would they want with the *Arcadia Queen?*"

"It does seem strange," Nancy agreed. "I mean, Cap could have wrecked it last night, if that was what he wanted to do. Did you have a chance to ask him what he was doing there?"

"Not yet," Mrs. Newcomb replied. "I've been completely swamped with last-minute preparations for an outdoor exhibit of figureheads that's going on display. I'm afraid I haven't had a spare minute to track down Cap. Considering the way he and Vincent seem to feel about me right now, I doubt I'd get a straight answer out of either of them, anyway, even if I did try to talk to them.

"What about the students in the program?" Mrs. Newcomb asked, changing the subject. "Have any of them been acting suspicious?"

When Nancy told her about how Deke Ryan had been acting, Mrs. Newcomb frowned. "If Deke *is* the culprit, we're going to be in a very sticky situation," the seaport director said. "The Ryans are a very influential New England seafaring family. Generations of Deke's ancestors owned and captained sailing ships around the world. His family has donated thousands of dollars to the seaport, as well as many valuable antiques."

"I guess they wouldn't appreciate hearing about their son getting in trouble here when they've given so much to the seaport," Nancy said.

"Right," Mrs. Newcomb said, grimacing. "I had a serious talk with Deke after Cap kicked him out of sailing class yesterday. He promised to be more respectful in the future, but of course he didn't give any clue that he could be behind the sabotage to the seaport."

"George and I will do our best to find out who the culprit is—whether it's Deke or someone else," Nancy promised. "Tomorrow I might not be able to get much investigating done, though. I'm going to be out all day on the *Seafarer*."

Mrs. Newcomb nodded. "Cap is going to be along on that trip. I believe Vincent is going, too. He said something about seeing how the *Seafarer* sails after a repair job he just finished on one of the masts."

"Great," Nancy said, brightening. "Then I'll be able to keep an eye on both of them and Deke."

The director gave Nancy a concerned look. "Just promise me you'll be careful."

"I will," Nancy assured the director. "With all of our suspects in one place, I ought to be able to find out *something* useful! I'll let you know."

"Mmm, this salty air smells fantastic!" Claire said, inhaling deeply.

"I'll say," Nancy agreed. She felt an exhilarated rush as the *Seafarer* rose up over a swell, then dipped down the other side. Wind filled the long ship's three large sails, occasionally blowing sea spray into her face. The coastline was just a distant blur to the west.

Nancy couldn't help wishing that George could be with her—she knew her friend would love it. All of the students seemed excited to be out on the ocean. They were even acting a little friendlier to Nancy, but she had the feeling that they still didn't completely trust her.

The students had been divided into three groups—one to act as the sailing crew, one to perform marine experiments, and a third to learn navigational techniques. Nancy, Claire, Tom Chin, and a black-haired boy named Julio had already studied navigational techniques. Now they were in charge of handling the sails. Nancy and Claire manned the wheel while Tom and Julio made sure the sails were set at just the right angle. Cap had supervised them closely at first. Now that they'd gotten the hang of sailing such a large ship, he just watched from a distance.

Nancy's eyes drifted toward the middle section of the boat, where Mr. Vilander, their marine science teacher, was preparing to drop a two-foot-long glass and metal instrument over the side to collect a sample from the ocean bottom. Deke was among the group, Nancy noticed. For once he didn't seem to be acting up—he simply watched along with the others while Mr. Vilander demonstrated how to use the instrument.

So far Nancy had been too busy to find time to question Cap or Vincent Silvio. Then again, both of them had seemed completely caught up in their work, too. When Vincent Silvio wasn't busy checking the forward mast, he helped out Cap with the navigational and sailing crews. She hadn't seen either of them do anything suspicious, and so far there hadn't been any "accidents."

Nancy shivered as a stiff wind whipped over the bow, causing goosebumps to pop up on her arms. Glancing over her shoulder, she saw a bank of dark clouds on the western horizon.

"I hope that's not a storm headed our way," Claire commented, following Nancy's gaze.

"Me, too," Nancy agreed. She glanced down at her shorts and T-shirt. "I guess I should have dressed more warmly. I think I'll go belowdecks and get my sweater."

There was a raised cabin in front of the wheel, with a doorway and stairs leading down into the ship. Nancy ducked into the doorway and made her way down the steps. The third group of students was with Vincent Silvio at the foot of the steps, in a small room that contained sonar and other navigational equipment. Nancy quietly stepped around the group and made her way toward the room at the very front of the ship, which was crowded with small wooden sleeping bunks. That was where she and the other students had left their things.

She passed through the sleeping quarters for the ship's officers and into the galley. The motion of the boat was more confusing belowdecks, without the horizon to orient herself. As the boat took a particularly steep dip, Nancy had to reach out to the wall to steady herself.

"Careful, Drew," she murmured to herself.

64

Looking ahead through the open doorway to the front quarters, Nancy saw that a guy in a blue sweater was already there, rummaging through a knapsack.

He must be cold, too, Nancy thought. She was about to call out a friendly greeting when she got a closer look at the red knapsack—and stopped in her tracks.

The knapsack he was going through was hers!

8

A Sneaky Sailor

"Hey! That's my knapsack!" Nancy cried, stepping into the room.

The guy in the blue sweater quickly zipped up her bag, then whipped around to face her. Nancy found herself staring right into Deke Ryan's blue eyes.

"How's it going, Nancy?" he greeted her easily. He was gazing at her with the smug arrogance that she had come to know so well in him.

He has some nerve, Nancy thought, trying to act as if he hadn't been up to anything. But then, that was just like Deke. "You were going through my bag," Nancy accused him. "Why?"

"Who, me?" Deke asked, pointing at his chest and giving her a look of innocent disbelief. "I was just getting a pencil out of my own backpack, to take notes." He tapped a blue nylon bag that was resting right next to Nancy's knapsack, then pulled a yellow pencil from his jeans pocket.

Before Nancy could say anything else, Deke stepped past her and headed back toward the stairway leading to the deck.

Nancy glared after him. She was sure he had been looking in her knapsack, not the blue bag. Luckily, there wasn't anything in her bag to give away her real purpose at Bridgehaven Seaport. She'd brought just her sweater and a slicker in case of rain. She was willing to bet the blue bag Deke had indicated wasn't even his. Still, Nancy thought, as long as I'm here . . .

She glanced over her shoulder toward the galley. Seeing that the coast was clear, Nancy quickly unzipped the blue bag Deke had indicated. Inside was a jumble of socks and some orange plastic rain gear with his last name written on it in permanent marker. Nestled beneath the clothes was a copy of the maritime history text and a worn-looking, leather-bound booklet.

Nancy picked up the booklet and quickly flipped through it. It was some sort of diary that had been kept by a sailor out at sea. It was obviously very old—the pages were yellowed, and the dates of the entries were from the 1840s. Could Deke have checked out such a valuable old book from the library?

Nancy was going to look more closely when she was startled by footsteps out in the galley area.

Was Deke coming back? Nancy quickly slipped the diary into the knapsack again and zipped Deke's bag shut. Then she unzipped her own backpack, grabbed her sweater, and started back toward the rear of the ship.

"Oh, Nancy—there you are," Tom Chin said when she reached the galley. He was standing next to the table, biting into a slice of banana bread from a loaf that had been left out for the crew. "Cap sent me to look for you. He needs you to help us lower the sails so Mr. Vilander's group can drop a line to check the depth of the ocean floor."

"Sure," Nancy told him. She grabbed a piece of the banana bread for herself, and the two of them went back up on deck.

Looking toward the western horizon, Nancy saw that the thick bank of dark clouds was moving quickly their way. It now covered nearly half the sky, and flashes of lightning streaked down from it to the water.

As Nancy hurried back to help with the lines that controlled the sails, she glanced over at Deke. He had rejoined his group, and once again his attention seemed to be focused on Mr. Vilander. But Nancy had a feeling that despite his calm expression, Deke Ryan was someone who could be as dangerous as the worst thunderstorm.

"That storm was really hairy," Claire said, stepping out of the van three hours later. She pulled up the hood of her orange slicker to protect herself from the lightly falling rain. "I'm beat."

"Not to mention soaking wet," Gayle added, pushing back a few damp strands of blond hair. "I can't wait to take a shower and get into some dry clothes."

The severe thunderstorm had overtaken the *Seafarer,* forcing the group to bring the boat in early to its dock at Newport, Rhode Island. The storm had slacked off to a gentle drizzle during the hour-long drive back to the seaport, but the weather was still gray and foggy.

Nancy was one of the last kids out of the van. Some of the students had already begun walking back to the student houses. Cap and Vincent Silvio stood a few feet away, looking after the departing orange, yellow, and blue slickers.

"A couple of raindrops, and they're all worn out," Cap muttered, shaking his head. "I'd like to see them out in the middle of a nor'easter. Then they'd know what a *real* storm is like. This group is hopeless!"

Nancy bristled as she reached for her red knapsack from the van's floor. She could understand Cap's disappointment at being forced to retire from captaining larger sailboats out on the ocean. But it wasn't fair of him to take his disappointment out on the students.

"Oh, those kids are all right," Vincent Silvio told Cap. "At least they're not trying to rob you blind all the time, the way some people do."

The bitterness in Silvio's voice was clear, but Cap didn't seem to pay any attention. "Well, it's been a long day," Cap went on. "I'm going to treat myself to a nice steak at Sizzlin' Jack's. Care to join me?"

Vincent Silvio declined, but Nancy's ears had perked up when she heard Cap's plans. She hadn't had a chance to really investigate Cap yet. He would probably be at the restaurant for at least an hour. That would give her plenty of time to check out the rooming house where he lived.

As the two men left, Nancy slung her knapsack over her shoulder. By now the last of the students had gone and Mr. Vilander was locking up the van. Saying good night to the science teacher, Nancy headed down Arcadia Street toward the rooming house where she and George had seen Cap two nights earlier.

When she reached the corner by George's house, she paused to look across at the rooming house. Although the sun hadn't set yet, the gray weather made it seem later than it was. Several lights were on in the two-story building, but Nancy was relieved to see that the room she had seen Cap come out of was dark.

"Here goes," she said under her breath. Nancy walked briskly to the outside stairway that led to the second-floor porch of the rooming house. Her feet squeaked on the steps, but no curious eyes peered out from any of the windows.

She made her way down the row of doorways, stopping next to the one she thought was Cap's. Her heart started beating faster as she peered in the window next to the door.

Inside, Nancy saw that the room was sparsely furnished, with a bed, a table, some books and seafaring memorabilia on a shelf, and a small desk. Cardboard boxes were stacked up against one wall, as if Cap hadn't unpacked all of his belongings. Nancy thought she recognized the blue work shirt hanging on the rack near the door. It was Cap's room, all right.

She reached for the doorknob—then froze as a voice spoke up loudly from below.

"Well, now, what have we here?"

With a gasp Nancy spun around. Cap Gregory was standing on the lawn below. His arms were crossed over his chest, and he was looking up at her quizzically.

Trying to ignore the pounding in her chest, Nancy groped for something to say. "Hi! I was, um, just looking for you." Her voice sounded falsely bright, even to her.

Luckily, she had a moment to collect herself while Cap climbed the wooden stairs to join her.

"So now that you've found me, what can I do for you?" he asked. He pulled a key from his pocket and unlocked the door, gesturing for

Nancy to come inside. "How did you know I live here, anyway?"

Nancy's mind searched for an explanation as she came inside and sat down at the table. "Well, I, uh, have to do this project for my maritime history class," she began, making her story up as she went along. "It's about sea chanties. Our teacher gave me your address. He thought you might have some information about old sea ballads that I could use."

Cap's expression immediately softened. "Well, I was on my way to dinner. Only came back because I wanted to bring a book with me. But I suppose I can spare a minute."

He moved to a bookshelf set into the wall behind his bed. After putting on his glasses, he examined the books and finally pulled one out. Then he sat down opposite Nancy at the table, opened the hardcover book, and showed it to her.

"I do love these old ballads," Cap said as Nancy flipped through the pages. They were smudged and well-worn, as if Cap used the book often.

"Can you tell me a little bit about the songs?" Nancy asked. "Did you sing sea chanties when you were out at sea?"

There was a look of longing in Cap's eyes as he gazed at the book of songs. "I certainly did. Sea chanties are the outpouring of a sailor's soul. In the old days sailors would be away from home for months, sometimes years," he explained. "These songs were a sailor's way of recording important events and expressing his love for the family he left behind."

As Nancy glanced at the songs, she was impressed by the stories they told. Some were love stories, others exciting tales of life on the high seas. Reading the lyrics made Nancy wish she was going to be staying at Bridgehaven Seaport long enough to really finish the project. But she hoped the mystery would be solved before then.

Nancy stopped at one page when she recognized the lyrics. "Hey, I heard this song down at the lighthouse the other day," she said.

Leaning forward, Cap glanced at the title. "Ah, yes. The story of the *Henrietta Lee*," he said, frowning. "It's not a very well known chanty, though. There are others you might be more familiar with."

He began to turn the page, but Nancy stopped him. At the lighthouse she hadn't had a chance to hear the entire song because it had been interrupted by the falling board. As she read through it now, she was intrigued by the words, which told the story of the *Henrietta Lee*'s shipwreck:

> In eighteen hundred and forty-three
> my bonnie Mary was waiting for me . . .

The beginning of the song was sad, about how there was no hope of being saved, and that the sailors—along with a cargo of gold coins being transported from South America—would be lost at sea. The sailor wept because he would never see his true love, Mary, again.

Nancy breathed a sigh of relief when she read the refrain, in which two sailors managed to escape in one of the lifeboats, along with the trunk of gold coins. They made it to an island where they buried the treasure, making a map to mark the spot.

But by that time the sailors were sick and nearly dead with fatigue. One of them actually died. The other sailor was afraid he would never make it back home alive, so he tore the map in two and hid the halves in the wreckage of the *Henrietta Lee*, which had washed up on the island.

As Nancy read on, the sea chanty took on a more playful tone. The sailor seemed to be giving Mary clues about where to look for the map halves:

> Oh, where to look, sweet Mary,
> where to search for my gold?
> You'll have to ask the barnacles
> growing on the hold.
>
> Oh, yes, sweet Mary,
> though battered and broken,
> my treasured *Henrietta Lee*
> holds the key.

Talk to the mice
scampering 'round the ship's clock.
They can tell you the answer, dear,
if only you'll ask.

Talk to the worms
that would eat at my writing desk.
They can tell you the answer, dear,
if only you'll ask.

Nancy blinked, looking over the last two verses again. A ship's clock had been taken from the whaling display, and a writing desk had been damaged on board the *Westwinds!*

A thought flashed into Nancy's mind. Maybe the acts of sabotage hadn't been intended to hurt the seaport. Maybe the person was looking for the map to the treasure from the *Henrietta Lee!*

9

Clue in the Sea Chanty

The more Nancy stared at the song, the more she was convinced that her theory was right. The saboteur had already gone after the ship's clock and the captain's writing desk, which were the first two items mentioned. Nancy's gaze moved to the next verse of the song:

> Talk to the eels
> that slither in the rigging chest.
> They can tell you the answer, dear,
> if only you'll ask.

"A rigging chest . . . that *has* to be the next target," Nancy murmured excitedly.

"Target?" Cap echoed. "I don't think this song mentions any target."

"Oh—I guess I, um, misread it," Nancy said, groaning inwardly at her slip. Giving Cap a big

76

smile, she asked, "Would you mind if I borrowed this for my project? It would really help me."

Cap hesitated, and a sudden thought occurred to Nancy. Cap had seemed reluctant for her to read the sea chanty about the *Henrietta Lee,* and now he seemed reluctant to lend her the book. Was that because *he* was using the song to try to find the map halves? But if so, why had he shown her the book in the first place?

"I'll be very careful," Nancy promised him. "I don't know where else I could ever find a book of sea chanties as good as this one."

"That's for sure," Cap said with a nod. He let out a breath, then handed the book to Nancy. "You can take this, but be very careful with it, young lady," he said sternly.

Nancy promised she would, then thanked Cap and rose to leave. Outside on the porch it was still misty and gray. Nancy saw that lights were on in the blue house where George was staying, across the street. She hurried down the steps. She had to tell George and Mrs. Newcomb about her discovery—the sooner the better!

Mrs. Newcomb let out a low whistle as she examined the book of sea chanties on her desk. "This is really something!" she exclaimed.

After leaving Cap's room, Nancy had gone directly to George's house and shown her the song about the *Henrietta Lee.* George had agreed that they should talk to Mrs. Newcomb right away. It was already after seven o'clock, but the girls had been lucky enough to catch the seaport director as she was leaving her office.

"I've heard this song before, but I never took it seriously," Mrs. Newcomb continued, shaking her head in disbelief. "You know, the ship was wrecked a few miles away from where the Arcadia River empties into the Atlantic Ocean. It happened back in the 1840s. I just assumed that if there *was* a treasure, it would have been found long ago."

"Well, someone is taking the song seriously enough to ruin some valuable things here at the seaport in order to find that map," George said.

"We have to do all we can to protect the seaport against any more damage," Nancy added.

George nodded. "At least we have a list of the things that might be targeted now. So far, the attacker has been going after the items in the order they appear in the song."

Mrs. Newcomb bent over the book again, sliding her finger down the page to the third hiding place mentioned. "A rigging chest," she mused. "Let me see if the seaport has the one from the *Henrietta Lee.*"

Mrs. Newcomb turned on her computer and typed in some commands. "Here's a list of everything we have that was salvaged from the *Henrietta Lee,*" the seaport director said. "The descendants of one of the ship's officers donated quite a few things from the wreck about ten years ago."

Leaning across the desk, Nancy stared at the glowing amber print on the computer screen. "Look! A ship's clock is one of the items," she cried.

"And a captain's writing desk," George added.

Mrs. Newcomb was gazing at the list on the computer screen. "What do you know," she said. "The seaport *does* have the rigging chest from the *Henrietta Lee*. It's on display in our rigging loft."

"Sounds logical," Nancy said. Turning to George, she added, "I hope you didn't make any plans for tonight, because we've got a mission."

"Aye, aye, sir—I mean ma'am," George responded with a grin, making a quick salute. "Let me guess. We're going to stake out the rigging loft, right?"

"You got it," Nancy told her. "It's a long shot. Our saboteur might not even show up there tonight. But it's all we have to go on."

Turning to Mrs. Newcomb, Nancy asked, "Is there any way someone else could get this information? Whoever's been sabotaging these things seems to know exactly where to look."

The seaport director nodded. "The material can be accessed from the computer in the library," she explained. "We installed the system so that people doing research could find anything at the seaport related to their subject."

As Nancy gazed back at the sea chanty on Mrs. Newcomb's desk, an idea suddenly occurred to her. "I think we have to add another suspect to our list," she told George and Mrs. Newcomb.

"Who's that?" George asked.

"Claire Roebling. She's doing her maritime history project on the *Henrietta Lee*. She could have found that song when she was doing research for her project," Nancy explained. "That could explain why she's always studying."

"You mean, maybe she's reading books and stuff about the *Henrietta Lee* to try and figure out where the treasure is?" George asked.

Nancy shrugged. "Maybe." She looked out the window. "It's going to be dark pretty soon, so I think we should get over to the rigging loft. Can you tell us where it is, Mrs. Newcomb?"

Mrs. Newcomb gave the girls directions. "I'm going to alert security that you'll be there, but I'll ask them not to stay too close to the building," she said. "If our saboteur sees a guard, he or she might run away before we have a chance to see him. And tonight I'll check my own personal library to see if I can find information about the shipwreck that might be helpful."

"Thanks," Nancy said. For the first time since she and George had arrived at Bridgehaven, she felt that they were really onto something. With any luck, they would catch the culprit before the night was out!

* * *

80

"This place is *so* cool," George whispered fifteen minutes later.

The rigging loft was located in a two-story building near the lighthouse. The girls had paused inside the door to let their eyes adjust to the darkening night. Now Nancy could make out a large collection of coiled ropes, fishing nets, wooden pulleys, and tools that were arranged along the room's four walls. The center of the room was empty, except for a table and workbench.

"It's amazing, all right," Nancy agreed. She stepped into the room, breathing in the scents of hemp and wood that filled the air.

"Look, that must be the rigging chest," George said in a low voice, pointing to the only trunk in the room. Placed on the floor to the left of the door, its wooden planks were weathered and covered with gouges and nicks.

"Let's see if the map half is in it," Nancy said excitedly, hurrying over to the chest.

The two girls examined it using a flashlight that George had brought from her house. Ten minutes later George sat back on her heels with a disappointed sigh. "Nothing," she announced. "I hope the saboteur hasn't already been here."

"I doubt that he or she has," Nancy said. "So far, the person has always damaged something before leaving. Nothing here seems to have been touched."

George gazed curiously at Nancy. "Doesn't it

seem strange that the person keeps wrecking the things he's searching?" George said. "I mean, it's as if he's advertising his treasure hunt."

"I don't understand it, either," Nancy said. "Come on, we need to find a spot to wait." She pointed to a staircase that rose up against the wall opposite the door. "The sign there says that the sail loft is upstairs."

Craning her neck, George looked up at the railing. "I bet we could hide behind that railing and still get a pretty good view of the rigging chest."

The two girls climbed the stairs. The dark, shadowy space at the top was punctuated by huge white triangles of sailcloth that were spread out on the bare floor. Nancy stepped carefully around the sail closest to her and went over to the railing. George was right behind her.

"Good, we can see the rigging chest perfectly," George said. "And it's dark enough up here that I doubt anyone will be able to see us. I just hope our person shows up. Otherwise, we'll be staying up all night for nothing."

"All we can do is wait," Nancy said softly. She rested her arms on top of the railing and propped her chin on her hands. Behind her, she could hear George moving around the loft.

A moment later a loud crash made Nancy whirl around. "George! Are you all right?" she asked.

George was sitting on the floor between two sails, rubbing her shin. A wooden bench was lying on its side next to her. "I'm okay. I just tripped on the edge of a sail," she said softly. "I was carrying this over to sit on."

Nancy hurried over and helped George to her feet. Together they carried the bench the rest of the way to the railing. They were just setting it down, when Nancy felt the hairs on the back of her neck bristle.

"Did you hear that?" she whispered to George, carefully scanning the rigging loft below.

George shook her head. The two girls stood for several long moments, watching and listening. All was still, except for the wind rustling through the trees outside.

"I guess it was just my imagination," Nancy whispered finally.

The two girls settled in on the bench. For over an hour the rigging loft remained quiet.

"My stomach is growling," George whispered. "I wish we'd thought to bring some sandwich—" She broke off as a creaking noise sounded out from the door below.

Nancy forced herself to stay completely still as the door opened. Even in the darkness she could make out the silhouette of the person who was entering. Although she couldn't tell who it was, the petite silhouette looked like a girl.

The person stepped into the rigging loft and began to walk slowly around. Nancy decided not to wait. She wanted to be as close to the rigging chest as possible when the person examined it.

Then maybe she and George could catch the culprit before any damage was done.

Tapping George's arm, Nancy gestured for her to follow, then began tiptoeing silently to the stairway. She barely dared to breathe as they made their way slowly downward, one step at a time. Luckily the person below didn't seem to notice. Nancy could hear her poking around.

Finally they were far enough down the stairs to see what the person was doing. Nancy heard George gasp as the dark silhouette bent over the rigging chest and pulled open the top. It was now or never!

"Hold it right there!" Nancy called. The person straightened up like a shot, letting the lid to the rigging chest bang closed. Nancy raced down the rest of the stairs, hurrying toward the silhouette before the intruder could get away. She could hear George's footsteps right behind her, but there was something else—a loud scuffling coming from the corner beyond the stairs.

"What—?" George's surprised voice came from behind Nancy.

Nancy turned, then gasped as a *second* shadowy figure rushed toward her and George. Before she could even move, the second figure hurled a bulky object straight at her and George. Nancy cringed as the object spread out in the air, swirling over them.

It was a net, she realized. And she and George were about to be trapped in it!

10

A Chase Through the Night

"No!" George's frustrated cry rang out from behind Nancy.

Nancy tried to dodge the net, but it was too late. She and George fell to the floor in a heap, tangled up in the heavy roped webbing.

Nancy looked up in time to see the figure by the rigging chest fly out the door. Then the second person, who'd thrown the net, raced across the rigging loft to the doorway and disappeared into the night. Nancy couldn't see the person's face, and a dark hooded windbreaker hid his hair. From the figure's broad-shouldered build, she was pretty sure it was a guy.

"Quick! We've got to go after him!" she told George, pulling at the net. Within seconds they worked themselves free, and Nancy jumped to her feet.

"I'm right behind you, Nancy!" George said.

Outside, Nancy caught sight of a black shape racing past the Student Training Building, near the lighthouse. She and George took off in pursuit. They were only about twenty yards behind him, and they were gaining.

Suddenly the black shadow veered left and headed for an extremely long, low building across from the Student Training Building.

"He's going in," George said breathlessly, drawing even with Nancy. "What's in there?"

"I don't know, but we're about to find out," Nancy replied without slowing.

She and George were only about ten yards away as the person pulled open the door at one end of the building and disappeared inside. Moments later Nancy threw open the door, and she and George raced in after him. The door banged shut, echoing around them.

The two girls stopped, blinking into the darkness. Nancy didn't hear the other person at all now. The only sounds came from her and George as they tried to catch their breath.

Nancy saw that the building stretched out for hundreds of feet in a long, narrow space. A faint glow from the lamps outside the building filtered in the small windows along the sides of the building. Tall racks stood on either side of her and George, each holding about a dozen large spools.

"That's hemp," George whispered, sniffing the air. She pointed to the dark tendrils that unwound from each spool. The threads wove together in a shadowy network of ropes that seemed to stretch endlessly down the long building, at about waist level.

"This must be the rope walk," George added. "It's how they used to make rope in the old days—they twisted the smaller sections of rope together all the way down the building. Some of the guys at the shipyard told me about it."

Nancy couldn't see the rope clearly—it all melted into a black mass farther down. But she knew that whoever they were chasing had to be around somewhere, and she wasn't going to let him get away.

"Come on," she whispered to George.

The ropes stretched down the middle of the building, with clear areas on both sides. Nancy started slowly down the right side, while George took the left, shining her flashlight in front of her. Nancy listened carefully for any sound, but there was none except their own soft footsteps.

As they continued down the long room, Nancy saw that three smaller ropes fed through a machine that twisted them into a larger rope. She half expected to see their attacker crouched behind the machine, but there was just empty space.

"Hey!"

George's shout made Nancy jump. Several feet in front of her, George's flashlight illuminated a figure bolting from behind a huge coil of rope.

Pulling his hood close around his face, he ducked beneath the twisted hemp and headed toward a window at the far end of the building.

Nancy and George immediately took off after him. But before they could reach him, he pushed up the window and slipped through to the outside. By the time Nancy got through the window herself, the person was nowhere in sight. He had disappeared in the maze of seaport buildings.

"We lost him!" she cried, letting out her breath in a disappointed rush. "I can't believe he slipped through our fingers again."

George's head appeared in the window Nancy had just climbed through. "I couldn't tell who it was, even with the flashlight," she said, climbing out to join Nancy. "What happened back there, anyway? Who threw that fishing net at us?"

"The person we were just chasing, I think," Nancy answered. She dragged the toe of her sneaker in the grass while she replayed the scene at the rigging loft in her mind.

"Remember I thought I heard something after you fell with the bench?" she said.

George snapped her fingers. "That's right! So the guy who threw the net at us must have come in then and hid by the stairs, where we couldn't see him." She frowned at Nancy. "But how could he have known we'd be there—or why? I mean, if he wanted to stop that other person from wrecking the rigging chest, then why did he go after *us?*"

Nancy had been wondering the same thing. "It's almost as if he didn't want us to catch whoever came after the rigging chest," she said slowly. "But I don't have the slightest idea why. If he wanted the map half, he could have just looked for it himself. And he obviously knew *where* to look, or he wouldn't have been in the rigging loft in the first place." She frowned as another thought occurred to her. "Unless he followed us there from Mrs. Newcomb's office."

"I don't know about you, Nancy, but my brain is on overload," George said, leaning against the building. "We have too many questions and not enough answers. I say we call it a night."

"I guess you're right," Nancy agreed, making a frustrated stab at the grass with her sneaker.

"Hey, what's that?" George asked, shining her flashlight at Nancy's foot.

Glancing down, Nancy saw that she had accidentally uncovered a folded sheet of paper with her sneaker. She bent down to pick it up. "It's dry, even though it's been raining this evening," she told George. She unfolded the note as she spoke, a wave of excitement running through her. "I bet whoever we were chasing dropped this by mistake in his hurry to get away."

George leaned closer, shining her flashlight on the paper. "It's a photocopy," she said. "Looks like a list of books."

"And check out which ones are circled," Nancy said. She pointed to three entries that had been marked with red ink. "Two of these are books about the *Henrietta Lee!*"

"But what about that last one—'The personal diary of Jack Benbow,'" George read from the list. "Who's he?"

Nancy's crinkled up her forehead, thinking. "I give up," she finally said. "I guess I'll have to wait until tomorrow, when I can look him up in the library. Let's go back to your house so I can pick up my knapsack. And then I'd better get back to the house before my housemates think I dropped out of the program."

"Hi, stranger," Rochelle greeted Nancy as she walked in the front door twenty minutes later.

Rochelle, Evelyn, and Gayle were sitting in the living room in their nightgowns and bathrobes. They were all drinking tea and eating cookies from a plate on the coffee table. Nancy didn't miss the curious looks that they gave her.

"This is really a day for disappearing acts," Gayle said slowly. "First you never come back after our sailing trip, and then Claire takes off."

"I can't believe she'd still be at the library," Evelyn added. "Even Claire can't work *that* hard, not after a whole day out at sea."

Nancy looked at her housemates in surprise. "Claire's been gone all evening?" she asked.

"Ever since dinner," Rochelle replied.

Nancy's mind was racing. The figure she'd seen bending over the rigging chest had been petite—

90

about Claire's size, now that Nancy thought about it. Maybe her theory about Claire looking for the treasure from the *Henrietta Lee* was right!

Trying to act casual, Nancy headed for the stairs. "I really need a hot shower," she told her housemates. "I'll be back down in a minute."

It wasn't a complete lie. She *did* need a shower, but first she wanted to look through Claire's things. As soon as she got to the room she shared with Claire, Nancy locked the door. Then she sat down on her bed and looked around.

Apart from the two beds they each had a small desk and a few drawers in which to store their belongings. Nancy kept her clothes in a dresser against the wall, and Claire used the four drawers that were built into the bottom of her bed. They shared the closet, so Nancy doubted she would hide anything in there. The only thing on the wall was a nautical chart of the area around Bridgehaven Seaport.

Nancy went over to Claire's bed, knelt down, and opened one of the drawers. She felt around the neat piles of shorts and jeans but didn't find anything suspicious. The second drawer was also very neat, containing some sweaters and sweatshirts.

When Nancy opened the third drawer, however, she was surprised to see a messy jumble of T-shirts. She reached her hand down into them and started to feel around.

A moment later her hand clunked against

something hard and metallic. She quickly pushed aside the shirts—then gasped.

"I don't believe this," she whispered, staring into the drawer.

There, among the jumble of different-colored shirts, was a brass ship's clock!

11

Claire's Story

Nancy's mind was reeling. So it *was* Claire who had stolen the clock!

Still, something didn't make sense to Nancy. Claire really seemed to love everything about Bridgehaven Seaport, yet some of the damage to the seaport had been brutal and senseless. Nancy had a hard time believing that Claire could be responsible for the shredded lining of the captain's writing desk or the carved graffiti Mrs. Newcomb had described. On the other hand, she knew from other cases she'd solved that greed sometimes made people do terrible things. Perhaps Claire's love for the seaport was all an act.

Picking up the heavy brass clock, Nancy took it over to her desk and looked at it closely. She felt certain that Claire had stolen it in order to search it for one of the map halves mentioned in the sea chanty about the *Henrietta Lee*. Sure enough, the screws that attached the front of the clock were loose, as if Claire had unfastened the front to check inside.

Nancy was intent on loosening the clock face when she heard the doorknob rattle. Claire! Before Nancy could put the clock back in Claire's drawer, a key scraped in the lock and the door opened. Claire walked in, pulling off her rain slicker and shaking her damp black curls. "I can't believe how wet everything—"

She stopped short when she saw what Nancy was holding. For a long moment the two girls just stared at each other.

"I know you've been looking for the map to the treasure from the *Henrietta Lee*," Nancy finally said.

Claire's blue eyes darted nervously around the room. "How dare you go sneaking through my stuff," she snapped. "It's private!"

"Stolen is more like it," Nancy said dryly, holding up the ship's clock. "You can drop the innocent act, Claire. I saw the sea chanty about the *Henrietta Lee* and the buried treasure. I don't think it's a coincidence that the things mentioned in it are the same ones that have been vandalized here at the seaport." She held up the clock. "I think you're the culprit."

Claire's blue eyes flashed angrily as she took off her wet slicker and hung it on the closet doorknob. "You probably did the damage yourself, and now you're trying to blame it on me!"

What is going on here? Nancy wondered. Why was Claire acting so righteous, when Nancy had proof that she was guilty?

She decided it was time to level with Claire. "Claire, I think you should know that I'm not really a student—I'm a private investigator. Mrs. Newcomb asked me to come here to find out who is responsible for the damage. You can call her if you don't believe me."

Claire's eyes widened in surprise. "Hey, you can't nail this on me. Maybe I did take the clock, but I didn't wreck any of the other stuff."

"How could that be?" Nancy asked, shooting her roommate a probing look. "Maybe you'd better start at the beginning."

Claire went over to her bed and flopped down on it. Grabbing her pillow, she punched it into a tight ball in her lap. "When I came here I didn't know anything about the *Henrietta Lee*, much less about the treasure," she said. "I was amazed when I first read about it for my maritime history project. I mean, the captain nearly died trying to save the crew and the ship. He was lost at sea for two days before they found him, sick with pneumonia, at the foot of the Arcadia River."

"Where did you read about the shipwreck?" Nancy asked.

Claire went over to her desk and picked up two

slender books, which she showed to Nancy. Both were about the *Henrietta Lee*. "They mostly talk about the ship's streamlined design and its importance as a commercial schooner. There's only one little section on the shipwreck. The information came from the *Henrietta Lee*'s captain—he was the only one who survived the wreck."

Nancy eagerly skimmed the text Claire showed her. It mentioned that a trunk of gold coins was lost at sea when the crew perished. There was nothing about the coins having been buried, or about a treasure map.

"At first I just assumed that the gold coins were lost for good, or that someone had found them long ago," Claire went on. "But then, when I came across the song with all those clues in it, I couldn't resist checking it out. Believe it or not, I actually found one of the map halves in the very first place I looked, the ship's clock."

"That's amazing!" Nancy exclaimed, shaking her head.

"I thought so, too, until . . ." A fearful glimmer came into Claire's eyes. "Nancy, something really creepy is going on," she whispered.

"What are you talking about?" Nancy asked, blinking in surprise.

Claire took a deep breath before answering. "Someone has been following me," she began. "It started the night I took the ship's clock. I was really scared about sneaking into that display, but

I didn't plan on stealing the clock. I was just going to open it up there to see if the map was inside. But I heard someone coming before I could look, so I took the clock and ran.

"I thought it was a guard, but the next day when I heard that the display had been trashed, I knew it had to be someone else," Claire went on. "Then, when I went to the *Westwinds* to look for the captain's desk, I heard someone up on the deck before I even had a chance to look. That's why I took off like that. I was terrified."

Nancy nodded thoughtfully. "Someone else was in the rigging loft tonight, too," she put in. "They tripped up my friend and me so we couldn't catch you."

Claire's eyes widened. "I practically had a heart attack back there!" she exclaimed. "I didn't know what was going on, but I was sure someone was coming after me."

"It looked to me as if the person was trying to protect you, not harm you," Nancy said. "He didn't want us to catch you, that's for sure. Do you have any idea who it could be?"

"I don't know. Maybe the same person who" —Claire hesitated, running a hand through her black curls—"the same person who stole the map half from me."

"What!" Nancy exclaimed, leaning forward in her chair.

Claire nodded miserably. "I kept the map half

in a notebook in my desk drawer," she explained. "But when I got back from the library last night, it was gone!"

This case was getting more complicated every second, Nancy realized. "You didn't tell *anyone* about your search?" she asked.

"No one," Claire assured her. She shot Nancy a nervous glance. "And that's the way I'd like to keep it. Nancy, you *can't* tell Mrs. Newcomb what I did yet," she begged. "There's no way she'll believe I *didn't* wreck anything until we find the person who did. She'll kick me out of the program!"

Nancy thought for a moment. "I'll tell you what," she said. "I won't say anything—if you promise to back off looking for the treasure."

"Oh, Nancy, I can't," Claire objected. "Finding the treasure is like the ultimate challenge of my maritime history project. I really want to show everyone that I can find it on my own—you know, to leave my own special mark on maritime history."

She looked imploringly at Nancy. "As soon as I find the treasure, I'll turn it over to the seaport, I swear."

"It's too dangerous," Nancy insisted. "At least until we find the person who's been causing all the damage around here. Claire, you have to promise not to tell anyone else the real reason I'm here."

For a moment Nancy thought her roommate

might refuse. Finally Claire sighed and said, "It's a deal."

Claire got up from her bed and went over to her desk, where she pulled a notebook from her top drawer. "After the map half was stolen, I tried to draw everything I could remember from it," she said, handing the notebook to Nancy. "You'd better take it. If I keep it, I'm afraid I won't be able to resist looking for the treasure."

"Thanks," Nancy told her. "Oh—one more thing," she added, thinking of the photocopied list she and George had found outside the rope walk. "Does the name Jack Benbow mean anything to you?"

Claire nodded. "He was the first mate of the *Henrietta Lee*," she replied, a gleam of interest in her eyes. "Do you think he had something to do with the treasure?"

"I don't know. That's something I'm going to have to find out," Nancy said determinedly.

While Nancy opened the notebook, Claire took her bathrobe from the closet, then headed for the door. "After all I've been through today, I really need a shower," she said. Then she paused and looked at Nancy.

"Thanks for being so understanding," Claire said quietly. "Actually, it's a big relief to get all this stuff off my chest."

"No problem," Nancy told her. "Let's just hope we find the person who took that map half soon."

After her roommate had left, Nancy examined Claire's re-creation of the map half. The map indicated some water and part of a small island with half an X on it. Next to the map was the notation "Lat. 41.43 N."

That had to be the latitude of where the treasure was buried, Nancy figured. But without the longitude, Nancy didn't see how she could locate the little island. Chances were, the longitude was indicated on the other map half.

Looking up from the drawing, Nancy let out a sigh of relief. This mystery was far from being solved, but at least some of the pieces were starting to fall into place.

"See you guys in class!" Nancy called over her shoulder to her housemates the next morning.

The others were still eating breakfast, but Nancy had already finished. She had gotten up early so that she could stop by the shipyard before maritime literature class. Nancy knew her housemates would probably be suspicious of her early departure, but she had to tell George everything she'd found out from Claire.

The weather was still gray and damp. A light drizzle fell, and fog shrouded the whole street. She could see only about twenty feet in any direction. Even though Nancy was wearing jeans and a long-sleeved shirt under her raincoat, she felt a little chilly.

She carefully made her way to the end of her

road, then down Arcadia Street. After a few minutes the Bridgehaven Seaport sign appeared out of the fog, and Nancy turned into the entrance. She was glad that she knew her way around the seaport fairly well. Even without being able to see everything, she easily found the path that led to the shipyard.

When she reached the entrance of the large building, George was standing just a few yards away. She was nervously fingering the leather work belt strapped over her jeans, and there was a very distraught expression on her face.

"Nancy!" George hurried over as soon as she saw her. "I'm so glad you're here. I was just about to call you at your house."

Nancy swallowed the nervous bubble that rose up into her throat. "What's wrong, George?" she asked.

"Vincent Silvio just had a total fit," George explained. "He's furious at Patricia Newcomb."

A quick glance around the shipyard told Nancy that Silvio wasn't there. "Where is he now?"

"I'm not sure," George replied anxiously. "First he said something about how Mrs. Newcomb isn't going to get in his way this time. And then he just took off."

George took a deep breath, then added, "He was carrying a pretty sharp tool—a caulking iron—and waving it around like a weapon. Nancy, I think something terrible is about to happen!"

12

Stop Him—Before It's Too Late!

"We've got to go after him, George!" Nancy said urgently. "When did he leave?"

"Just a second before you got here," George replied. She unstrapped her work belt and tossed it over by the lockers. "We might still be able to catch him. Let's go!"

Nancy and George hurried outside. In the thick fog it was hard to see much. Nancy focused all her energy on trying to distinguish the hazy shapes around them. "In this fog Silvio could probably do a lot of damage without anyone seeing him," she whispered.

"At least the seaport isn't open to the public until nine," George put in. "That's not for fifteen minutes, so there aren't any tourists to confuse us."

"Or witnesses, if he does something awful," Nancy added, frowning.

As the girls stepped away from the shipyard, Nancy quickly filled in George on her confrontation with Claire the night before.

"You're kidding!" George exclaimed in a low voice. "So she's the one who—" She broke off and pointed. "Nancy, there!"

Nancy could make out the lighthouse to the left, its powerful beam of light cutting through the mist. She started as a sudden movement near the building caught her attention. A dark silhouette was moving hurriedly past the lighthouse, toward the docks.

The two girls took off in pursuit. As they drew closer, there was no mistaking Vincent Silvio's muscular build. Nancy could just make out a slender instrument clenched in his right hand.

"Where's he going?" George wondered aloud.

"I'm not sure, but wherever it is, we're going to be right there to make sure he doesn't do any damage," Nancy said firmly.

She and George kept a slight distance back, following Silvio along the docks. Soon the antique sailing ships were visible on their left, their masts no more than blurry lines in the mist.

Vincent Silvio crossed the gravel path next to the docks, heading for a familiar wood-shingled structure. "Isn't that the building where we saw Cap the other night—you know, the one with the display from that boat?" George whispered.

"The *Arcadia Queen*," Nancy supplied. "The

model we saw Silvio holding at his house was of the *Arcadia Queen,* too."

George gave Nancy a confused glance. "So what's the connection with the treasure from the *Henrietta Lee?*" she asked.

"Beats me," Nancy replied. She picked up her pace as Silvio reached the building and went inside. "Maybe Mrs. Newcomb is in there—or one of the items that was salvaged from the *Henrietta Lee.*"

Suddenly George grabbed Nancy's arm, pulling her to a stop next to a piling at the end of the dock. "Check it out," she whispered. "It looks like Vincent Silvio isn't the only one interested in that display."

Nancy's eyes widened as she saw Cap Gregory approach the building from the opposite direction. He didn't appear to see Nancy and George. After looking left and right, Cap opened the door and went inside.

"It looks like my suspicion that they're working together was right," Nancy whispered urgently. "Come on!"

The two girls bolted across the gravel path, threw open the door to the shingled building, and ran inside. Nancy immediately saw that Cap Gregory and Vincent Silvio were at the far end of the display, huddled over something.

"Hold it!" George called out. "Don't lay a finger on that!"

Nancy hurried over to the two men. She shivered when her gaze fell on the sharp, chisellike instrument Vincent Silvio held, but she couldn't let him destroy the beautiful display. Up close she saw that he and Cap Gregory were next to the captain's quarters of the *Arcadia Queen*, bent over the intricate wood paneling.

Cap Gregory and Vincent Silvio both straightened up in surprise. "George, shouldn't you be back at the shipyard? What's going on?" Silvio demanded, glaring at Nancy and George.

"We might ask you the same question," Nancy said. She nodded at the metal instrument in Silvio's hand. "Is that what you used to wreck the whaling display?"

Silvio looked down at the caulking iron, then back at Nancy and George. "I didn't have anything to do with that." He glowered at Nancy and added, "You're the troublemaker I saw up in the lighthouse the other day. I don't know what you two are up to, but—"

"We're not the ones who are up to something," George put in, her hands on her hips. "We happen to know that you took a model of the *Arcadia Queen* from the seaport's collection, Mr. Silvio."

"And we saw you sneak in here the other night, Cap," Nancy added. "Why would you snoop around if you're not out to do some damage?"

Cap and Silvio exchanged a long glance. "I guess we'd better confess our terrible crime to these landlubbers, Vincent," Cap finally said. He

105

crossed his arms over his chest and chuckled as he gazed at Nancy and George.

"There's nothing funny about this," Nancy said, bristling. Apparently Cap and Silvio didn't know how much trouble they could be in.

Vincent Silvio shot Nancy and George a leery glance. "Did Patricia Newcomb put you up to this?" he asked, shaking his head angrily. "She's doing it again—she's trying to steal my design!"

"Calm down, Vincent. I don't think Pat is behind this," Cap said, raising a hand. Turning to Nancy and George, he added, "Not that it's any of your business, but if you must know, the reason we're so interested in the *Arcadia Queen* is that I want Vincent to design a boat for me to live on, and I want it modeled after the *Queen.*"

George gazed dubiously at the two men. "That's all? But then, why are you two sneaking around?" she asked.

"Patricia Newcomb has already stolen enough of my designs," Silvio sputtered, angry red spots coloring his cheeks. "If she knew about this, she'd be sure to find a way to steal this project from me, too."

From all Nancy had seen since arriving at Bridgehaven Seaport, the only one who thought Mrs. Newcomb was stealing designs from Vincent Silvio was Silvio himself. Nancy couldn't be sure there wasn't more to their story, though. The two men might also know about the treasure from the *Henrietta Lee.* The board had been pushed from the lighthouse at the beginning of the sea chanty about the *Henrietta Lee,* as if someone didn't want anyone to hear all of the clues to finding the map halves. Silvio could have pushed the board. And Cap *had* been reluctant to lend her the book of sea chanties containing the song.

Nancy asked the two men a few more questions, but neither of them seemed to take the tale of the treasure very seriously. After making an apology, she and George left.

"Talk about embarrassing," George said under her breath as they walked away from the building.

"Well, at least now we know why those two have been acting so secretive," Nancy said. "It's frustrating, though. We've been here for over three days already, and we still don't know who's been damaging the seaport's displays!"

After her morning classes Nancy went to the main room of the library to see what she could find out about Jack Benbow, the first mate of the *Henrietta Lee.* After setting down her knapsack on one of the three study tables in the center of the room, she hurried to the card catalog that stood against one wall.

From her back pocket Nancy pulled out the photocopy she and George had found the night before outside the rope walk. Nancy pulled open the drawer with the *B*'s.

"Benbow," she murmured as she thumbed

through the cards. "Here it is—Jack Benbow." According to the listing, he had written some kind of diary.

She then checked the other listings that had been circled on the photocopied sheet. They were the two historical accounts of the *Henrietta Lee* that Claire had shown her—Nancy knew they wouldn't be in the library. After writing down the library call number for the diary, she took it to the librarian and asked to take out the book.

A few minutes later Nancy was sitting at one of the long tables, looking at a photocopy of Jack Benbow's diary.

"Hey, wait a minute," Nancy murmured excitedly as she read through the first pages. It was the same diary she'd seen in Deke Ryan's bag on board the *Seafarer!* Deke had had the original leather-bound copy, Nancy remembered. Could the seaport library have photocopied it in order to have more copies available? She hadn't seen a library card for another copy. Nancy made a mental note to ask the librarian before she left.

Now that she had more time to examine the entries, she realized that it was a diary of the day-to-day activities on board the *Henrietta Lee*. She skimmed through to the final entries, which were made in November of 1843.

"'In eighteen hundred and forty-three, my bonnie Mary was waiting for me. . . .'" Nancy quoted the first line of the song about the

Henrietta Lee's shipwreck. This diary was probably from the ship's last, fateful voyage, she realized.

She flipped back, carefully reading over the entries from the beginning of that trip. The first mate's account confirmed what Claire had told her about the captain of the *Henrietta Lee*, Decatur Preston, having been a great man who was loved by his men. The last entry was written during a storm, but there was no mention of the ship being in danger, or of a treasure.

Too bad that doesn't help me figure out who stole the map half from Claire, Nancy thought to herself. With a sigh she got up and went back to the librarian's counter. "Does the seaport have the original of Jack Benbow's diary?" she asked as she handed over the photocopy.

"I don't believe so, but let me check." The librarian turned to a computer terminal on the counter. "No, I'm sorry, but this copy is the only one the seaport possesses," she told Nancy.

Nancy's mind was filled with questions as she thanked the librarian and left. Where could Deke have gotten the original diary from? And what was he doing with it? Could *he* be the person who had been following Claire?

Nancy paused on the path. She had a feeling there was some clue to the *Henrietta Lee*, or Jack Benbow, that she was missing. Maybe Mrs. Newcomb had found more information on the *Henrietta Lee* in her personal library. Nancy started briskly down the path that led to the director's office.

The sound of rapid footsteps on the wooden dock behind her made Nancy pause. She turned her head in the direction of the steps, but in the thick fog it was impossible to see who it was.

Before Nancy could open her mouth to ask who was there, a bone-chilling scream rang out from somewhere behind her.

13

A Cry for Help

Goosebumps rose up on Nancy's arms and legs. A split-second later the scream was followed by the splash of someone hitting the water.

"Help!" a familiar voice called out amid sputtering and coughing.

"George!" Nancy cried. Spinning on her heel, she raced back toward the dock. Within moments the dock pilings appeared out of the mist, and Nancy glimpsed the choppy, blue-gray water of the Arcadia River beyond. She didn't see George but could hear her thrashing in the water to the left.

Nancy raced down the dock, all her senses on red alert. As she drew closer to the *Westwinds* she finally spotted her friend. George was swimming toward a ladder at the side of the dock. Her bulky rain slicker, jeans, and shirt were getting in her way, causing her to move with stiff, thrashing strokes.

"Are you all right?" Nancy called, hurrying over to the ladder and giving George a hand up.

"I'm okay." George gave Nancy a sober look as she climbed onto the dock. "I decided to take a walk along the docks before going back to the house for lunch. Nancy, someone just ran out of nowhere and pushed me into the water!"

Those must have been the footsteps she'd heard, Nancy realized. "Did you see who it was?"

George shook her head, giving a frustrated tug at her slicker as she tried to free herself of the clingy, rubberized material. Once she had peeled it off, she started squeezing water from her jeans and shirt. "He hit me from behind. By the time I surfaced, the fog was so thick I couldn't see him. I'm pretty sure it was a guy, though. At least, it sounded like a guy's voice."

"He said something?" Nancy asked.

George looked nervously around, then said in a low voice, "I think he pushed me as a warning for us to back off the case. I was splashing so much that I didn't hear every word, but I'm pretty sure he said something about how I'd better leave the seaport—and take my friend Nancy Drew with me. He couldn't have been far away, but with the fog and everything, I didn't see him."

Nancy pressed her lips together in a grim line. "You could have been seriously hurt, George. I

112

feel awful." She carefully scanned the dock area, but the fog was still too thick to see much.

"I don't like this," she went on grimly. "First someone cuts the rigging on the whaling ship so that I'd fall, and now this. . . ."

Angry red blotches colored George's cheeks. "Well, whoever it was can't scare us away that easily!" she insisted.

"The question is, who was it?" Nancy asked. "I suppose it's possible that Cap Gregory and Vincent Silvio are up to something a lot more sinister than they let on this morning."

"They seemed pretty sincere, Nan," George said, sounding doubtful. "What about that guy on your program—Deke somebody?"

"Deke Ryan," Nancy supplied. "He *was* going through my bag on the *Seafarer* yesterday. He also had a diary from the first mate of the *Henrietta Lee*. And he could have cut the rigging on the *Benjamin W. Hinton*. His group went up right before mine, and he even stood right where I did."

"Not to mention that he brags about being in the seaport at night," George added. "He could be the one we chased in the rope walk. And I bet he ruined that portable writing desk, too." Running a hand through her dripping curls, George gave Nancy a meaningful look. "After this, I think you'd better put him at the top of your list of suspects."

"I'm definitely going to check him out more

thoroughly," Nancy agreed. "But first I want to take a look at Mrs. Newcomb's personal collection of maritime books. I keep thinking that there's some clue I'm missing in the story of the *Henrietta Lee.* If I can just find out more information about that last trip, when the treasure was lost, maybe we can figure out who's behind all the attacks."

"Good luck," George said, picking up her slicker. "I'd better head back to my house and change out of this stuff. It was embarrassing enough facing Silvio after chasing him into the *Arcadia Queen* display this morning. I don't think he'll be too thrilled if I show up back at the shipyard and start dripping water all over everything."

"I'll keep you posted, George," Nancy said. "See you later."

When Nancy reached the Administration Building, the secretary told her that Mrs. Newcomb was out at a meeting of the seaport's board of directors. Nancy left a note asking the seaport director to contact her, then left.

Back outside Nancy checked her watch. She only had fifteen minutes before that afternoon's woodworking workshop at the shipyard. She'd have to hurry if she wanted to eat lunch beforehand.

Nancy made her way down the misty paths toward the student entrance to the seaport. She passed the general store, rounded a corner, then paused.

The open square in front of her was filled with a dozen carved wooden statues, about six or seven feet tall. Nancy knew from her classes that they were called figureheads and that they used to be fastened to the very front of old sailing ships.

"These are amazing," Nancy whispered aloud. She stepped up next to a carving of a woman in a long, flowing robe, standing on a moon. Although the paint decorating the figurehead was faded and chipped, Nancy could still see the determined, inspiring expression on the woman's face. It was as if she embodied the spirit of the men who sailed her boat, spurring them on to new horizons.

Nancy couldn't resist taking a moment to stare at the impressive figureheads. They were all quite different. Next to the woman was an Arabian soldier, attired in colorful clothing and holding up a curved saber. Then Nancy moved on to a pair of roly-poly twins and a man in an officer's uniform. A small signpost set up next to each figurehead listed its age and the name of the ship it had been on.

Nancy was looking at a carved unicorn figurehead when a sudden thought occurred to her. Hadn't the sea chanty from the *Henrietta Lee* mentioned a figurehead in one of its verses? She closed her eyes but couldn't recall all the words to the song.

It was a long shot, but maybe that figurehead was right here! A rush of adrenaline spurred Nancy the rest of the way through the exhibit. Three figureheads from the end, she found what she was looking for.

The figurehead for the *Henrietta Lee* was also a woman. The wooden locks of her blond hair had been carved to look as if they were blowing out behind her. In one arm she held a telescope, while the other reached out in front of her, as if beckoning to the wind.

Nancy walked around the figurehead, trying to see any spot where a piece of map might be hidden. It looked as if the figurehead had been carved from a single piece of wood. The wood was worn and covered with minuscule cracks, but none of them looked big enough to hold even a small piece of paper or parchment.

Then Nancy's gaze fell on the woman's left arm. On second glance she saw a tiny seam at the shoulder. The arm and torso were actually made of separate pieces of wood, very carefully fitted together. If she could just loosen the joint and peek inside . . .

Nancy was relieved to see that the area around the town square was empty. The weather seemed to have kept the tourists away. Turning her attention back to the figurehead, she tried to delicately twist its wooden arm away from the shoulder. The arm didn't budge.

Gripping the arm more tightly, she gave it a

firm tug. With a loud squeak, the arm budged just a fraction—but at least it moved. Working as quickly and carefully as she could, Nancy kept twisting the arm until at last it came free of the rest of the figurehead.

She saw that the arm had been attached by a thick wooden peg that now stuck out of the figurehead's torso. A hole had been carved out of the arm at the joint, so it could fit over the peg. Nancy hardly dared breathe as she looked into the cavity.

The wood was old and cracked, and splinters had come loose as a result of Nancy's tugging. The yellowish brown square beneath the bits of wood had been so compressed by the pressure of the joint that at first Nancy thought it was just a discoloration in the wood. But when she reached in and flicked at the edge of the square with her nail, she realized that it was a piece of parchment!

Ever so carefully she pulled the parchment square from the wooden cavity and unfolded it.

"I don't believe this," she whispered, staring down at the crude drawing. It was covered with faded, old-fashioned markings.

She had found the other half of the treasure map!

14

The Missing Map Piece

Nancy stared in amazement at the map half. She was so caught up in the old drawing that she began to lose all sense of where she was or what time it was.

As she had suspected, this map half indicated the longitude of the spot where the treasure was buried, 71.82 W. Nancy was sure that if she matched this longitude with the latitude marked on the other map half, that would tell her the location of the islet.

Nancy turned her attention to the markings on the islet itself. A dotted trail started at the shoreline, from what looked like a huge rock. Markers for the treasure hunter to use as guidelines were indicated along the dotted line. Her pulse started to race when she spotted the other half of the X. This map showed most of the small, peanut-shaped island, with notations in old-fashioned script. "'Twenty-five paces south, then left at tortoise rock,'" Nancy read aloud in an amazed whisper. "'Curve right at split oak tree.'"

Even though Nancy knew she had to turn the map halves over to Mrs. Newcomb right away, she couldn't help feeling intrigued. She didn't approve of the way Claire had sneaked around and broken seaport rules, but she understood the lure of the search. In her mind Nancy could picture a gleaming pile of gold coins. She was even tempted to go look for the treasure herself!

A noise from the general store tore Nancy from her daydream. Suddenly alert, she whipped her head around in time to see an orange blur disappear around the side of the building.

"Hey!" Nancy called out. She started after the person, then changed her mind. She couldn't just leave the figurehead from the *Henrietta Lee* in two pieces. Besides, in this fog she doubted that anyone who wasn't right next to her could even see what she was holding.

After carefully refolding the parchment map half, Nancy tucked it inside the copy of *Moby Dick* she'd brought to her maritime literature class that morning. She twisted the wooden arm back onto the shoulder, then stood back to examine it. The figurehead looked exactly the way it had when she first saw it.

Nancy was so lost in thought that she hardly knew how she got back to her student house. She was relieved to find that her housemates had already left for that afternoon's demonstration at the shipyard.

Her stomach was growling, but she was too excited to eat anything. Taking the stairs two at a time, she went directly to her room. After retrieving the map half Claire had re-created, Nancy fitted both halves together on her desk. Now she could see that the islet where the treasure was located was near the mouth of a river. Based on what Mrs. Newcomb had told her, Nancy felt the river had to be the Arcadia.

Getting up from her desk, Nancy hurried over to the nautical chart of the area around Bridgehaven and brought it back to her desk. Luckily the chart included the area just off the Connecticut coastline. Three small islands were clustered in the offshore area near the Arcadia. A grid of fine lines was superimposed over the map, indicating latitude and longitude.

Nancy's heart pounded in her chest as she found the latitude and longitude indicated on the parchment map halves. "Forty-one degrees, forty-three minutes north, seventy-one degrees, eighty-two minutes west," she murmured. She ran her fingers along each line, to the spot where they intersected.

"Bingo!" she exclaimed. Her fingertip was on

Hawk's Isle, the middle islet of the three near the mouth of the Arcadia. It was vaguely peanut-shaped, just like the one indicated by the parchment map.

Nancy shook her head in disbelief. Was it really possible that a treasure had been hidden so close to the seaport all these years?

She took a deep breath, thinking of what her next step should be. Obviously, she had to go to Mrs. Newcomb with the treasure map as soon as possible. But it bothered her that she still didn't know who had been sabotaging the seaport and following Claire. Nancy realized that if she didn't find the real culprit, Claire would probably take the blame.

So far it looked as though Cap Gregory and Vincent Silvio were in the clear. But there was one person Nancy still hadn't had an opportunity to investigate: Deke Ryan.

Nancy glanced at her watch. Everyone in the student program would be over at the shipyard now, at the woodworking workshop.

"I think a visit to Deke's house is in order," she murmured, thinking out loud. If a search of his room didn't turn up anything, then she would go straight to Mrs. Newcomb with the map.

From downstairs Nancy heard the front door open and close. Who could that be? she wondered uneasily, scrambling to hide the map halves in case the person came up to her room.

"Hello? Nancy, are you here?"

Nancy let out a relieved breath. "Upstairs, George," she called back.

George's ruddy face appeared in her doorway a moment later. As she entered the room, Nancy saw that she had changed into a dry pair of jeans and a sweatshirt.

"When I didn't see you over at the shipyard with the other students, I thought you might be onto some big lead," George said. "Silvio told me to take the afternoon off when he heard about my getting knocked in the water. After this morning I guess he didn't really want me around, anyway," she added with a chuckle.

She let out a low whistle when she saw the parchment map half in Nancy's hand. "Is that what I think it is?" George asked, hurrying over to Nancy's desk.

Nancy nodded. Quickly she explained how she had found the map half and showed her friend Hawk's Isle on the nautical chart.

"Wow!" George shook her head in amazement. "No wonder you didn't go to the woodworking workshop. Finding a treasure beats sanding down a bunch of planks any day."

"Actually, I wasn't going to go after the treasure yet," Nancy said. "We still have to find out who's been sabotaging the seaport."

George nodded. "I guess thinking about the treasure made me forget all about that," she said with a grin. Then her expression grew more serious. "Did you have a chance to check out Deke yet?"

"I was just about to go over to his house," Nancy told her.

Raising an eyebrow at Nancy, George said, "Well, you know what they say—two snoops are better than one."

"Definitely," Nancy agreed, laughing. Reopening *Moby Dick*, she placed the parchment map half, plus Claire's drawing of the other half, between two pages. Then she closed the book and slipped it into her bottom desk drawer.

"It ought to be safe there until we get back," she said. "There's another thing I have to do before we go, too."

"What's that?" George asked.

"I have to grab a sandwich," Nancy said. "I'm starved!"

Fifteen minutes later Nancy and George were approaching a green house with a gabled roof that was two houses up the street from Nancy's student house. A stiff breeze had come up, lifting the fog from the area. Even though it was still very hazy out, she could see clearly up and down the street.

The front door was locked when Nancy tried it. "Mmm," she said, glancing around. "I bet they have a spare key around here somewhere. . . ."

Her gaze fell on a potted plant hanging from the eave right next to the door. Reaching up, she felt the dirt around the plant. Her fingers touched something metallic, and she pulled it out.

"Good going," George said approvingly as Nancy held up a brass key. "Now let's hurry and get inside before the neighbors call the cops."

The inside of the house had the same lived-in look as Nancy's student house. The furniture in the living room, just off the front hall, looked worn but comfortable. Sweaters, books, and sneakers were scattered everywhere.

There was a stairway to the right, and the girls took it up to the second floor. Four doorways lined the hall. A quick look revealed that they led to a bathroom and three bedrooms.

"I guess we won't have much trouble figuring out which room is Deke's," George said dryly, flicking a thumb at the door closest to the stairs. A hand-printed sign on the door read The Deke Machine and Chin-meister—Enter at Your Own Risk!

Entering the room, Nancy and George took a quick look around. There were two desks in the room, one set against the wall next to the door, and the other beneath a window against the opposite wall.

"There's probably something in these desks to tell us which one is Deke's," Nancy said.

"I'll check out the closet," George told her. "If I find the other map half, or anything that could be connected to the attacks, I'll yell."

While George opened the closet door, Nancy went over to the desk nearest the door. The desktop was littered with candy wrappers, some letters, and a messy pile of schoolbooks. Glancing at the letters, Nancy saw that they were addressed to Deke Ryan.

One of the letters was unfolded and written in a looping, feminine script.

"Dear Deke," the letter began. "Your father and I miss you. . . ."

Nancy skimmed over some news of Deke's younger sister and brother, then read more carefully as the letter turned back to the subject of the seaport: "I am so proud to see you carrying on the fine sailing tradition of our family. If only your great-great-grandfather, Decatur Preston, could see you now! I know that . . ."

Nancy stopped reading. Her eyes were fixed on the name of Deke's relative. The realization hit her like a bolt of lightning.

Deke's great-great-grandfather had been the captain of the *Henrietta Lee!*

15

The Secret of the Henrietta Lee

"George, look at this!" Nancy cried.

Nancy showed her friend the letter and explained Deke's connection to the captain of the *Henrietta Lee.*

"If Deke knew about the *Henrietta Lee,* he must have heard about the treasure, too," George said.

"Which means that Deke must be the one who stole the map half from Claire!" Nancy finished.

"What about all the sabotage?" George asked. "We still don't have proof that he's responsible."

Turning back to the desk, Nancy opened the top drawer and began rummaging among the pens and papers. "There has to be proof here somewhere. . . ."

The top drawer didn't seem to hold anything incriminating. Nancy was about to close it when a tiny yellow-brown fleck caught her eye.

"Hey," she said, picking up the scrap and examining it. "This is a piece of parchment. It must be from the map half that was stolen from Claire." Nancy frowned. "There's only one problem—I don't see the map half anywhere."

"What about the other drawers?" George suggested. She opened the next drawer, which contained a disorderly pile of notebooks. George pulled them out, and she and Nancy began leafing through them one by one.

"Look at this," Nancy said, pulling out a faded pamphlet that had been wedged inside the cover of one of the notebooks. "This is the diary of the *Henrietta Lee*'s first mate, Jack Benbow. I saw it in Deke's bag on board the *Seafarer*, but I didn't know what it was then."

George leaned closer as Nancy opened the pamphlet and started skimming the pages. Most of the entries provided simple information—how far the ship traveled every day, what the weather was, any special sightings made by the crew.

"Wait a minute," Nancy murmured, staring at a page near the end. "I'm sure this entry wasn't in the photocopy of this diary that I read at the library."

She took a deep breath and began reading aloud: "'I have done a terrible thing. After three days of gale winds, a bolt of lightning struck the aft mast. The ship was lost.'"

A puzzled look came over George's face. "I

don't get it. I thought Captain Preston was the only one to survive the shipwreck. Jack Benbow must have lived through it, too, if he was able to write that. What was the terrible thing he did?"

"Benbow writes about that next," Nancy told her friend. " 'Captain Preston convinced me that it was our duty to save the chest of gold coins,' " Nancy read. " 'Ha! I know now that duty had nothing to do with it. We gave in to our greed. There was but one lifeboat, and Captain Preston and I used it to make away with the coins and our most treasured belongings. We left the crew to perish. . . .' "

"Oh, no! So Captain Preston *wasn't* a hero—he was a complete jerk!" George exclaimed, looking outraged. "And so was that Benbow guy."

Nancy skimmed ahead. "It looks as if Jack Benbow really regretted what he did, though. Listen: 'I am overcome by guilt. If I could exchange the gold coins for the lives of the crew, I would happily do it. It has been only a day since the wreck. We landed on an island late last night, and we are both sick with fever and chills. I don't know where we are, but I do not feel safe. Captain Preston has . . . changed. He shows no regret at having deserted his men.

" 'This morning I noticed that the forward half of the *Henrietta Lee* has lodged in the rocks just off this island. I cry every time I look at the wreck, but the captain shows no emotion. He

128

speaks of nothing but his newfound wealth. The greedy look in his eyes tells me that he means to share it with no one—not even me. I know now that I must get away from him quickly.'"

Nancy looked up at George. "That's the last line."

"Do you think Captain Preston killed him?" George asked, her brown eyes wide.

"Or maybe he died from his illness. We may never know for sure," Nancy replied, frowning. "All we *do* know is that no one ever saw Jack Benbow again. And even though Captain Preston survived, he certainly never told anyone about deserting his ship or taking the gold."

"He probably told everyone how he did his best to save the crew," George said, sounding disgusted. "That's what it said in those books Claire had, right?"

"I guess Captain Preston never made it back to get the treasure for some reason," Nancy added. "If he was sick, maybe he made the map and wrote the sea chanty so that his wife could go back and get the treasure if he died."

George frowned. "He must have hidden the map halves in the part of the ship that washed up on the island. But I don't see how he could make sure that his wife or anyone else would ever find the map, even if they found the song."

"If he was anything like Deke, maybe he *wanted* to make it really hard to find the map halves," Nancy said. "Maybe he thought that if he couldn't keep the treasure, he wasn't going to make it easy for anyone else to have it, either."

"There's still something I don't understand," George said. "I mean, if Deke is looking for the treasure himself, why would he protect Claire, the way he did in the rigging loft?"

Nancy shrugged. "Beats me, but I bet we'll find out soon enough," she said. "Once we show this stuff to Mrs. Newcomb, Deke is going to have an awful lot of questions to answer."

She slipped Jack Benbow's diary into the pocket of her jeans, along with the shred of parchment.

Being careful to leave everything as they had found it, Nancy and George left the house and replaced the front door key in the plant. Then they hurried back to Nancy's student house. Back in her room, Nancy went over to her desk.

Pulling open her bottom desk drawer, she took out her copy of *Moby Dick* and opened it, looking for the page where she had left the map halves. But when she flipped through the book, she didn't see anything.

Glancing at her desktop, Nancy realized that her books and papers were in a messy jumble, even though she'd left them in a neat pile. A feeling of dread welled up inside her as she searched through *Moby Dick* again.

"Oh, no!" she cried, staring at George. "Someone's taken the map halves!"

George's mouth fell open. "But how—?"

"We can't worry about that now," Nancy said urgently. Her mind flashed on the orange figure she had seen that morning by the figurehead exhibit. "I saw someone right after I found the second map half. It must have been Deke. He must have followed me back here . . ."

"And then waited until we left to sneak in here and take it," George finished. A look of horror crossed her face. "I'll bet he's going after the treasure right now!"

"We have to stop him," Nancy said, grabbing the nautical chart from her desk. "We can use this to get to Hawk's Isle. I think I can remember the markers that we have to follow once we get there."

It took only a few seconds to remove the chart from its frame. Nancy rolled it up and stuck it in the pocket of her slicker. Then she turned to George. "Let's go!"

"It looks as if Deke got a head start," George said as she and Nancy ran up to the Student Training Building five minutes later.

Nancy glanced at the row of sailboats outside the building. There was an empty space between two of the boats. "Maybe we can catch up to him before he gets to Hawk's Isle," she said, sprinting for the closest sailboat.

She and George hurried to place the boat in the water. Nancy glanced at the choppy gray sea.

The wind had lifted the fog, but now she could see a bank of dark clouds moving in from the north.

"I hope we can make it," Nancy said. "That islet isn't far from the mouth of the Arcadia River. If we're fast, we can probably beat that storm. Besides, if we wait, Deke might get away with the treasure!"

Within a few minutes the girls had started down the Arcadia River, with Nancy steering and George holding the lines that controlled the mainsail and jib. A stiff wind from the north filled the sails and whipped the girls' hair around their faces.

As the girls continued down the river, Nancy kept looking over her shoulder at the bank of clouds to the north. Just hold back long enough for us to get to Hawk's Isle, she silently begged. Still, every time she looked over her shoulder, the dark clouds were a little closer.

A half hour later she and George approached the mouth of the Arcadia River. The waves were even higher and choppier at the mouth, where the river met the Atlantic Ocean. The wind had grown stronger, too. It whipped the water into a frenzy of churning swells and whitecaps.

"Uh-oh." George frowned as the boat dipped sharply and a spray of water splashed across her face. "Looks like we're in for a bumpy ride!"

Nancy was too busy scanning the horizon to answer. Three gray shapes were visible—they had to be islands. Pulling the nautical chart from her slicker pocket, Nancy quickly consulted it, then gazed toward the horizon again.

"I'm pretty sure Hawk's Isle is that one," she said, pointing to the gray shape in the middle.

As Nancy steered toward the island, water splashed over the sides of the boat. Soon, she and George were both soaked. It took all of the girls' strength to keep the vessel from capsizing.

Nancy wasn't sure how they managed it, but forty-five minutes later they approached the small islet. From the sailboats it looked uninhabited. All Nancy could see was a small, rocky shoreline that gave way to a dense growth of trees, grass, and vines.

"Phew! I'm glad we're here. I don't know how much more torture these sails could take!" George called back to Nancy, speaking loudly to be heard above the whistling wind.

Nancy nodded her agreement. "I don't know how we're going to get back, but I guess we'll worry about that later."

When they were within a dozen feet of the craggy shoreline, Nancy pulled up the boat's rudder and George lowered the sails. Then the two girls jumped in and waded ashore, pulling the sailboat by its mooring line.

A huge boulder towered above the sand to the right, and Nancy saw a protected area behind it. She and George carefully carried the sailboat there, resting it gently in the sand. As Nancy straightened up, dusting sand from her hands, she noticed something sticking out from a thicket of bushes behind the boulder. It was the back of a sailboat hull.

"Looks like Deke is here, all right," she told George, nodding toward the other boat.

"At least he didn't leave yet," George said, scanning the dense woods. "Do you have any idea which way to go?"

Nancy gazed up at the towering boulder. "We landed at the right spot," she said. "I remember that the dotted line started at a huge rock. Now, what was it?" She closed her eyes and tried to visualize the map halves in her mind. "Twenty-five paces south, then left at a rock shaped like a tortoise," she said.

As the girls started into the dense woods, it was easy to see the tracks that Deke had left behind. The grass had been trampled down, and branches had broken off the nearby bushes.

"There," George said, pointing up ahead after about twenty steps. "That rock looks kind of like a tortoise."

Sure enough, it was oval, with a rocky knob sticking out at one end, like a tortoise's head. Nancy shot George an excited glance as they turned left. "Now we go until we see a split oak tree."

Deke had also turned left. As they followed the trampled-down path he'd left, Nancy gestured

134

for George to keep silent. She didn't want to give Deke a chance to get away.

A few minutes later George stopped and pointed ahead. "I think that's it," she whispered.

Peering into the woods, Nancy saw a wide oak tree whose trunk split into two arching branches and a canopy of smaller branches and leaves. It was an impressive tree, but she wasn't sure it looked old enough to have been alive over a hundred and fifty years ago.

She was about to say as much to George, when a noise coming from the woods to the right of the tree caught her attention. "That sounds like digging," she whispered to George.

The two girls moved as silently as they could toward the noise. As the steady, rhythmic sound of metal scraping against dirt grew louder and louder, Nancy felt her pulse begin to race. They were in luck! Deke hadn't found the treasure yet.

Nancy held her breath as she and George rounded a thick clump of vine-covered bushes. A moment later a bright orange rain slicker came into view. The person was hunched over a deep hole. Nancy did a double-take when she caught sight of the person's curly black hair.

"Claire!" she exclaimed, stepping forward. "What are *you* doing here?"

16

Treasure Hunt

"Oh, no!" Claire gasped when she saw Nancy. She dropped her shovel and stepped back uncertainly from the hole she'd been digging, a look of horror in her blue eyes.

George stepped up beside Nancy. "Unless Deke is into very clever disguises, I take it this isn't him?" she asked, eyeing Claire curiously.

Nancy was too surprised at seeing Claire to answer George's question. "So *you're* the person I saw when I found the second map half this morning," Nancy said to her roommate. Several students on the program had orange slickers, including Deke. Nancy hadn't made the connection that it might be Claire.

Claire nodded sheepishly. "I know I promised to stop looking for the treasure—and I meant to, honest," she began. "It's just that when I saw that

136

you'd found the other map half . . . well, I couldn't resist."

"So you followed Nancy," George put in. "And when she and I went to search Deke's house, you went up to her room and stole the other half of the map."

Claire's eyes flashed indignantly. "I'm the one who found out about this treasure in the first place," she said. "I deserve to be the one who gets the credit for discovering it! Who are you, anyway?" she added, frowning at George.

"She's a friend of mine who's helping me investigate at the seaport," Nancy replied.

The weather had worsened, she realized, glancing over her shoulder. Rain had begun pelting down, and the wind whistled loudly through the trees and bushes. "Claire, we don't have much time," Nancy added. "Are you sure this is where the treasure is buried?"

Claire rolled her eyes. "Of course I'm sure." She reached into her slicker pocket and pulled out the two map halves—one of parchment and the other the drawing she had copied from the map half that Deke had stolen. Taking the pieces, Nancy and George looked at them eagerly.

"Left at Tortoise Rock . . . right at the split oak . . ." George murmured, reading the flowery, faded script on the parchment map half. "Fifteen paces, and there's the *X*." She looked at Nancy. "I think she's got it, Nan."

"I don't know. You've already dug down over five feet," Nancy said, gesturing toward the deep hole. "Besides, I'm not sure that the oak tree we saw is the right one."

Claire looked at her doubtfully. "What do you mean?"

"It just doesn't seem like it could be a hundred and fifty years old," Nancy said.

"Now that you mention it, you could be right," George agreed. She gazed back in the direction of the oak tree. "Do you think we'll even be able to find the real one? I mean, a tree that old could have been totally destroyed by now."

"There's only one way to find out," Nancy replied. Picking up the shovel that Claire had dropped, she led the way back to the oak tree. Then she moved past it in a line that continued the path they'd made earlier, from the tortoise-shaped rock.

Claire peered dubiously into the dense undergrowth. "It doesn't look as if there are any other big trees near here." She let out a frustrated sigh, then burst out, "I'll just die if we don't find that treasure!"

Nancy was too busy concentrating on her surroundings to respond. As she walked, she looked from side to side, her eyes sweeping the rain-soaked bushes and trees they passed. Suddenly she stopped. "You guys—over there," she said, pointing up ahead.

George and Claire gazed at the raised, lumpy

patch of ground about six feet in front of them. It was completely covered with ivy that rustled in the stiff, wet wind. "What's so special about a clump of ivy?" Claire asked.

"I get it," George said, hurrying over to the raised area. "If an old tree fell down, and then ivy grew over it, it might look like this."

The three girls began tugging at the thick tendrils of ivy. "It *is* a tree!" Claire exclaimed, exposing a section of old, cracked wood.

"The question is, is it the right tree?" Nancy put in. She went to one end of the raised area and quickly pushed aside the ivy there. "This looks as if it was the trunk," she decided, staring down at the huge circle of decaying wood.

"So the part where the tree split would have to be up here somewhere," George added, stepping farther along the lumpy, ivy-covered area.

The three girls moved up the tree, clearing the wet ivy from it as they went. Nancy felt her excitement build with every inch they uncovered. All her instincts told her that this was the tree, but she had to see the split to be sure. . . .

"Aha!" Claire crowed. She pointed down at the section of the tree that she'd just uncovered. The trunk of the old, fallen tree separated into two large, distinct branches. "This is it!"

"Wow, I don't believe it," George murmured, staring down at the tree. "So now we go right—how many paces?" she asked, looking at Nancy.

Nancy consulted the map halves. "Fifteen," she replied.

The air buzzed with anticipation as the three girls paced off the steps. "Okay, let's start digging," Claire urged eagerly.

Claire took the shovel from Nancy and used it to clear the grass and ivy from the area. Then she plunged the shovel into the ground and tossed aside a huge clump of earth.

"I know it's a long shot that the treasure's still here after all this time, but this is really exciting," George said, her brown eyes gleaming.

Nancy had to agree. The three girls took turns digging the hole, which grew deeper and deeper. The rain continued to stream down, but they barely noticed it.

"I don't know," Claire said an hour later as she took over the shovel from George. "We've dug over four feet down, and we still haven't found the treasure."

"Maybe we got the directions wrong again," George said, brushing a wet strand of hair from her forehead.

"We can't give up yet," Nancy said. "Let's give it another ten minutes before we—"

Clank!

All three girls heard the metallic noise as Claire's shovel struck something hard. "I've hit something!" she cried. Dropping to her knees, she used her hands to brush the dirt from the top of the object. Nancy and George jumped down into the hole to help her.

Within moments they had uncovered the top of an oblong wooden trunk with worn leather straps.

"Wow!" Claire exclaimed. "We found it. We actually found the treasure!"

Nancy, too, was captivated by the sight of the old trunk. Could it really be the same treasure that had been mentioned in the sea chanty about the *Henrietta Lee* and in Jack Benbow's diary?

The girls went to work with renewed vigor, clearing the dirt from around the sides of the small trunk. It was extraordinarily heavy, but somehow they managed to drag it to the top of the hole and set it in the dirt there.

The three girls examined the trunk. Its leather straps were so worn that they fell apart at the slightest touch. Nancy saw that there was also a metal lock that had rusted shut. She grabbed a rock and banged it against the lock. Before long it, too, fell away.

"Here goes," Nancy said, shooting Claire and George an excited glance.

Together, the girls grabbed the lid of the trunk and tugged. At first it resisted. Finally the wooden lid creaked open with a loud groan. Nancy, George, and Claire all gasped at the same time.

Nancy had never seen such a brilliant sight. The trunk was filled to the brim with gold coins.

They were all different sizes and shapes, and they gleamed so brightly that she almost had to shield her eyes from the glare. For a long moment all she could do was stare at the coins, mesmerized. The only sounds came from the wind and rain.

"Amazing!" George finally exclaimed.

Just then a boy's voice spoke up from behind the girls, startling them.

"You three have done a great job."

"Deke!" Claire exclaimed, whirling around.

When Nancy turned, she saw that Deke Ryan had emerged from a thick clump of bushes a few yards away. As he walked toward the group, he stared at the gold coins with greedy eyes. She felt a cold stab of fear when she saw what he was holding.

It was a knife, and it was pointed right at her, George, and Claire!

17

A Deadly Surprise

Nancy tried to ignore the wave of dread that washed over her. George and Claire were both frozen beside her, their gazes focused on Deke's sharp knife.

"What are you doing here, Deke?" Claire finally spoke up.

Deke let out a short laugh. "I think the answer's obvious," he said. "I was waiting for you to find the treasure for me, of course."

"He must have followed us here, Claire," Nancy realized. She glared at Deke. "You've made a habit of that, haven't you? I know you're the one who followed Claire around and let her do your dirty work for you."

Deke didn't seem at all insulted by Nancy's accusation. "So what if I did?" he countered. "Why risk getting in trouble myself when Claire could do it for me?"

"*You* were the one in the rigging loft last night!" Claire exclaimed. "So you must have wrecked the whaling display and the captain's writing desk, too."

"Not to mention almost killing me by cutting the netting on the *Benjamin W. Hinton* so that I came close to falling on the whaling hook," Nancy added. "And shoving George into the river this morning."

When Deke didn't deny the accusations, Claire looked at him with a perplexed expression. "But why, Deke? If you wanted me to find the map halves, why did you ruin those beautiful things?"

Deke shrugged. "At first I wanted to find the map myself," he began. "My great-great-grandfather wrote that sea chanty about the *Henrietta Lee*. His wife, Mary Preston, found it in his writing desk after he died, not long after the *Henrietta Lee*'s shipwreck. He never did recover from the pneumonia he caught when the ship went down."

"Mary's the woman in the song," George recalled. "She was Captain Preston's wife?"

"Yeah," Deke replied. "You see, my great-great-grandfather owned the *Henrietta Lee*, so everything that was salvaged from the wreck was returned to Mary." He shook his head angrily. "Too bad my mother donated the clock and all those other things to Bridgehaven Seaport. If she'd kept them, I never would have had to come here in the first place."

144

Claire shot Deke an angry glare. "You don't care about the seaport at all," she accused. "Even if you just came to find the treasure, you didn't have to go wrecking everything!"

"I didn't plan to, but I was really mad when you beat me to the ship's clock, Claire," Deke explained. "That's why I wrecked the display you took it from. I couldn't believe it when you got to the captain's writing desk before me, too."

"So you wrecked it and then hid the tool you used behind the lockers at the shipyard," Nancy finished for him.

He nodded, turning his gaze back to the gold coins in front of the girls. "Then I got smart. I knew the only thing that really mattered was making sure I was around when you found the treasure, Claire. Which, as you can see, I've managed quite nicely."

Claire gasped. "Deke, you can't take this! It's not yours!"

"It belongs to anyone who finds it," he insisted. "Besides, it was originally my great-great-grandfather's, so rightfully it *should* be mine. It's my inheritance!"

"Your great-great-grandfather *stole* the treasure," George said indignantly. "He left his whole crew to die in that storm just because he was greedy. That's disgusting!"

In response to Deke's look of surprise, Nancy explained, "We found Jack Benbow's diary—the *real* one, not the photocopy from the seaport library. We read the last entries, where Jack Benbow reveals how he and Decatur Preston betrayed their crew in the storm that sank the *Henrietta Lee*. And I bet that once the treasure was safely here, Captain Preston killed Jack Benbow."

"Don't talk about my ancestor that way!" Deke snapped, spots of anger rising to his cheeks. "He was a great man—all the historians say so."

"But you know that's not the truth," Nancy said.

For a brief moment Deke looked uneasily from Nancy to George to Claire. "My mom couldn't bear to have people know what my great-great-grandfather did," he finally admitted. "So when she donated the diary to the seaport, she only gave a photocopy—minus the entries about him deserting his crew and taking the gold coins. She never even tried looking for the map halves mentioned in the song—she was too ashamed about what Decatur Preston had done to get the coins."

"What about the first mate?" George wanted to know.

Deke shrugged uneasily. "My parents never learned what happened to him. All we know is that my great-great-grandfather kept Benbow's diary after he died. Captain Preston took it to the mainland with him in the boat he and Benbow had taken from the *Henrietta Lee*. The boat had been damaged in the storm, and it was leaking.

146

Not to mention that my great-great-grandfather was still really sick. He was unconscious when some people found him near the mouth of the Arcadia. I mean, he almost died. It's not like the whole trip was a picnic for him, either," Deke finished defensively.

While Deke spoke, Nancy had been glancing around. Even though Deke was outnumbered, he had the advantage as long as he held that knife. She couldn't risk any of them getting hurt. If only she could find a way to disarm him!

"I think we've chatted enough," Deke said. A deadly serious look came into his eyes. "Now you're going to carry this trunk back to the shore," he ordered, gesturing toward the gold coins with his knife.

"We'll never make it to shore in this weather," Nancy said, trying to stall him. "We'd better wait until it stops."

Deke shook his head adamantly. "No way. In fact, the storm will be the perfect cover for what I have in mind."

"Wh-what's that?" Claire asked nervously.

"Oh, you'll see," Deke said vaguely, a mischievous smile playing over his lips. "I took a dolly from the seaport to carry the treasure. I want you three to get it, then move the trunk back to the shore. And remember—I'm right behind you."

Nancy exchanged a grim look with George and Claire. She didn't know how they managed it, but together they heaved the trunk onto the dolly.

147

The load of coins seemed impossibly heavy as they rolled it back in the direction they'd come from. The wind whipped at their faces, and hidden vines seemed to pop out of nowhere to trip them. By the time they finally reached the rocky beach where they'd left their sailboats, Nancy was breathless. Every muscle in her body ached from exertion.

"Phew!" George said, wiping the rain from her face. She glanced back at Deke, who followed with his knife trained on the girls. "Deke's certainly no gentleman," she muttered under her breath.

Nancy was too busy scanning the water to reply. Here on the open beach, she could see the full effects of the storm. The water was a raging mass of waves now. There was hardly any visibility.

"Deke, we can't go out in this storm," she called to him. "It's too dangerous!"

"Exactly," Deke said smugly. "When the Coast Guard finds the bodies of three girls, they'll assume it was an unfortunate sailing accident. . . ."

Claire gasped, looking at him in horror. "Deke! You don't really mean to—"

"Oh, yes I do," he said. "My motorboat is moored right behind that rock." He gestured toward the boulder Nancy and George had noticed earlier. "As soon as you three are . . . gone,

I'll get away in a flash. No one will ever know I had anything to do with it."

George looked nervously around. "Um, Deke, we'll get the trunk down to the water while you get your speedboat, okay?" she said. Nancy knew her friend was stalling for time.

"Not so fast," Deke said. "I can handle the trunk from here on. I think it's time you three went for a sail—to the bottom of the ocean."

Nancy fought down a wave of fear as Deke bent to pick up a large rock from the beach. What was he planning?

"Deke, you can't just k-kill us in cold blood!" Claire pleaded, her voice a fearful wail.

Nancy shivered at the evil gleam in Deke's blue eyes. He stepped toward them, the rock in one hand and the knife in the other. "Oh, yeah? Just watch me," he said. "After you three are knocked out, I'll tow you and the sailboat behind the motorboat. Then, when we're far enough from the island, I'll dump you overboard."

Nancy couldn't believe how cold and calculating Deke was. She didn't doubt that he meant every word.

All of a sudden Nancy thought she caught a glimmer of light out on the water. Because of the storm, it was hard to tell for sure, but . . . Yes! There it was again. It was a boat!

A quick look at Deke told her that he hadn't seen the light. If she could just disarm him, they

149

could yell for help. But as Nancy's gaze fell on the rock and knife he held, her heart sank. She didn't see how they could jump him without running the risk of getting seriously injured.

The sudden blast of a foghorn made Nancy jump. Deke was taken by surprise, too, and he whipped his head around to stare out to sea.

In that second Nancy leapt into action. She covered the distance to Deke in two long strides, then lashed out with a judo kick that sent his knife flying.

Deke was too stunned to say anything but "Hey!"

"I'm with you, Nancy!" George called out. Before Deke could react, George caught him in a flying tackle, while Nancy retrieved the knife from the sand. Claire jumped to George's aid. Within seconds they had Deke's arms pinned behind his back.

"Good work, guys," Nancy said. "Now, we've just got to get that boat's attention."

Keeping a strong hold on Deke, who was struggling and crying out, the three girls started screaming for help at the top of their lungs. A moment later they saw the boat's strong spotlight cut through the storm toward them. Then a faint, amplified voice echoed over the water: "This is the Coast Guard . . ."

"I still can't believe you guys actually found a trunk of gold coins that's been buried for over a

150

century and a half," Rochelle said the following afternoon.

She, Nancy, George, Claire, and the rest of the students from the summer maritime program were gathered around a grill on the dock outside the Student Training Building. The entire seaport had been buzzing with the news of the treasure and Deke's treachery ever since the Coast Guard had brought back Nancy, Claire, and George the day before. The weather had cleared, so Mrs. Newcomb decided that a barbecue would be the perfect way to celebrate the girls' discovery and the end of the case. A smoky scent filled the air, making Nancy's stomach growl.

"It *is* amazing," Mrs. Newcomb added, while Rochelle brushed sauce on the fish fillets on the grill. "I'm just relieved that you all made it safely through yesterday's storm."

"No thanks to Deke Ryan," Tom Chin said. He frowned down at the plate of barbecued fish and potato salad he held. "If I had known how twisted that guy was, I never would have become friends with him. I'm glad he didn't get away with the treasure—or with hurting anyone."

"When Cap reported that some of the boats were missing, he had a feeling something awful had happened," Mrs. Newcomb went on. "It's a good thing he had the sense to call the Coast Guard."

Rochelle handed Nancy a plate of fish and salad, and she dug into it with gusto. "Deke

151

really thought he had a right to that treasure—
no matter what he had to do to get it," Nancy
said, shaking her head. "Now that he's been
arrested, he'll have a long time to think about
how wrong he was."

"I know I've learned *my* lesson," Claire put in.
She had been standing next to water, looking out
over the Arcadia River, but she joined the group
in time to hear Nancy's comment. "Mrs. Newcomb, I'm so sorry about breaking into the seaport's displays and taking that clock. Thank you
for giving me a second chance."

After hearing Claire's story, the seaport director had decided to let Claire off with a stern
warning. "I can't say I approve of what you did,"
Mrs. Newcomb said, "but Nancy told me of your
intention to turn the treasure over to the seaport.
Besides, the ship's clock from the *Henrietta Lee* is
back in the whaling display now. And you *did*
help to capture Deke. . . ."

"What's going to happen to the treasure, anyway?" Tom Chin interrupted, looking curiously
at Nancy.

Mrs. Newcomb grinned at Nancy, George, and
Claire. "Legally, sunken treasure belongs to the
person who finds it," the seaport director said.
"Or in this case, the three people. But Nancy,
George, and Claire have decided to donate the
treasure to a worthy cause."

"We voted unanimously to give the gold coins
to Bridgehaven Seaport," George explained. "Af-

ter all, the treasure and the story of the *Henrietta Lee* are an important part of the history of this area. It seemed right that the money should go to the seaport, since Bridgehaven is totally devoted to teaching people about our sailing history."

"The treasure map and the wooden chest the coins were found in will go on display here at the seaport, along with a few of the coins," Mrs. Newcomb added, a pleased smile lighting up her face. "By selling the rest of the coins to dealers and collectors, we'll be able to raise millions. We'll have enough money to keep Bridgehaven Seaport going for a long, long time."

As the others continued to talk about the treasure, Nancy's gaze roamed over the dock area. She was surprised to see Cap Gregory and Vincent Silvio round the side of the training building. They were talking animatedly about something.

"How's the design for your new boat coming along?" Mrs. Newcomb asked as the two men stepped up to the group. "Though I guess we all know that if *I* were designing the boat, the result would be a lot nicer," she teased.

Silvio's face reddened with anger. "That's a bold-faced lie!" he exclaimed. "There's no way I'll discuss the plans with you. You'd just steal this design from me, too! Sorry, but you'll have to wait until she's built, like everyone else."

"Good enough," Mrs. Newcomb replied with a laugh.

EAU CLAIRE DISTRICT LIBRARY

"I guess the competition between those two is as strong as ever," George whispered to Nancy.

Nancy chuckled, taking a bite of her grilled fish. "At least Mrs. Newcomb has agreed to let Cap keep the boat here at the seaport once it's built."

She turned as Cap came up beside her, a smile on his wrinkled face. "An old man hates to admit to making a mistake, but I guess I had you pegged all wrong, Miss Drew," he said.

"What do you mean?" Nancy asked.

Cap rubbed his chin before answering. "Well, when you first got here, I didn't think you could sail a toy boat in a mud puddle," he began. "But anyone who could make it to Hawk's Isle in the kind of weather we had yesterday—and find a treasure to boot—is okay in my book."

"Thanks, Cap," Nancy said, smiling back.

"I agree," Mrs. Newcomb added, stepping up to Nancy, George, and Cap. "You two would make a couple of fine skippers. Bridgehaven Seaport is going to miss you!"